USA TODAY BESTSELLING AUTHOR

Dale Mayer

TERKEL'S TEAM SERIES

SCOTT'S SUMMIT

BOOK 06

SCOTT'S SUMMIT: TERKEL'S TEAM, BOOK 6
Beverly Dale Mayer
Valley Publishing Ltd.

ISBN-13: 978-1-773365-24-4
Print Edition

Books in This Series:

Damon's Deal, Book 1

Wade's War, Book 2

Gage's Goal, Book 3

Calum's Contact, Book 4

Rick's Road, Book 5

Scott's Summit, Book 6

Brody's Beast, Book 7

Terkel's Twist, Book 8

Terkel's Triumph, Book 9

About This Book

Welcome to a brand-new series from *USA Today* best-selling author Dale Mayer, where dark-ops SEALs have special senses and skills, needed to solve intrigue, betrayal, and … murder. A series with all the elements you've come to love, plus so much more, … including psychics!

Everyone has the right to make a mistake, … but the one Naira made isn't one Scott can forgive. He wakes from a coma, sure that the ex-love of his life had been at his side, but finds no sign of her. When he does see her, he can't get past a long-ago decision she'd made that tore them apart.

Naira had hoped that Scott would protest her decision way back when, but he didn't say anything to stop her. Heartbroken, she went ahead with the business marriage to appease her father, which ends in divorce. When Terk called, she came running to Scott's bedside, even knowing he'd hate to see her when he woke up. But she has always loved him and can only hope he might find his way back to her.

But finding his way back to the team is on his mind, with Naira second. Except that the operatives who took down his team initially are coming around and trying to pick off everyone left alive—and all the people they hold dear, … like Naira.

Sign up to be notified of all Dale's releases here!
https://geni.us/DaleNews

PROLOGUE

S COTT WOKE UP. His gaze was fuzzy; his eyes ached, and he didn't recognize anything around him. The woman sleeping in the chair beside him though, that was someone he knew. He blinked several times to be sure. "Naira?"

She bolted to her feet and raced to his side. "Hey. How are you?"

He drifted back under without answering; just knowing that she was here was incredible. It felt like he'd been climbing through the clouds to get back to her for a very long time. There was another woman though, a woman whose name evaded him, and that bothered Scott because he felt like she was important, and he didn't know who or how she fit into things, but Naira was here, and that mattered in a way that he couldn't even explain. He heard voices dimly in the background, and he tried hard to focus, but he couldn't.

Another voice whispered in his consciousness. *Relax. You've made the big jump. Now just calm down and rest.*

Scott kept fighting toward consciousness, and, when it wouldn't work, he felt himself panicking. A gentle touch reached out, stroked his forehead, and he was out cold.

When he woke the next time, he didn't know what was going on, but more awareness was slowly returning. Had he just dreamed that Naira was here? He opened his eyes, and, sure enough, she sat at his bedside again. He stared at her.

"What are you doing here?"

And damn if his voice didn't sound like it was rocks in the water, gravelly and yet soft.

She bounced to her feet. "Terk told me that you were here and that you were hurt."

Scott noted a little nervousness in her voice and her gaze. He closed his eyes again. "You're not supposed to be here."

"I know," she admitted in a low voice, "but I couldn't stay away."

He tried to open his eyes, but, once again, he went under.

When he woke the next time, he was alone, and he hated to say it, but it was a relief in itself. He wasn't sure what he had seen before, but no way Naira should have been here. She was married, with a husband and a whole different life, one that didn't include Scott. He rested for a moment and then slowly shifted in the bed, searching, looking around. He didn't know where he was.

Almost immediately the door opened, and Terk stepped in, along with another woman. Thankfully it wasn't Naira. Scott wouldn't mention Naira's presence either, since it would show where his mental state was, and he couldn't afford that. The woman stepped forward, placed a hand on his forehead, and he determined she was a nurse, although she didn't wear the traditional scrubs.

She smiled at him. "My name is Cara. How are you feeling?"

He stared up at her, feeling a recognition that he didn't quite understand, but he nodded. "I think I'll live."

"Good." Terk stood beside him. "We've been waiting a long time for you to come back."

Scott stared at his old friend. "How long?"

"Over a month," Terk replied. "A few days longer, I guess."

Scott's gaze widened. "I've been out that long?" he asked in alarm.

Terk nodded. "And you'll slowly recover. You know what happens when your body has been incapacitated for that long. It'll take some time to recuperate."

"Well, I'm sure you probably have some magic juice to help me get back on my feet faster," he murmured. "The nightmares are the worst." He shook his head. "God. It's almost enough to stop me from going back to sleep."

"We can't have that." Cara stood at his side. "Rest is what you need, and rest is what you'll get."

Something was in her tone. He looked at her. "As long as you don't do anything to force me back to sleep again because I've had some of the roughest nightmares ever."

"Not at all," she replied gently, "but you do need to rest, and you do need to sleep."

"Maybe." He yawned, looked around. "Where's everyone else?"

"Most of the team are back on their feet," Terk noted. "I hate to say it, but you're one of the last few to surface."

He stared at him. "Seriously? Even as strong and fit as I was?"

"You also took part of that blast a little harder than anybody else."

"I don't even remember what happened." But he felt the need to sleep taking over again. "I'd go back to sleep right now but for those damn dreams."

Immediately Cara put her hand on his forehead and said, in a gentle voice, "Sleep."

And just before he lost consciousness, he whispered,

"Was she here?"

"Was who here?" Terk asked, his voice low.

He whispered, "Naira. Was she here?"

Scott waited desperately to hear the answer, only to go under—the question left unanswered.

CHAPTER 1

S COTT LITTLE OPENED his eyes and stared around the room, frowning.

When an older woman walked in, she gave a startled exclamation and then smiled brightly. "You're awake."

He nodded slowly. This was not the gifted nurse accompanying Terk earlier. He remembered her coming to him two times. *Cara.* In his thoughts and in reality. "If that's what you call it, yes," he replied. "I feel like I got hit by a sledgehammer."

"And maybe you did at that," she agreed, with a bright smile. "However, a lot of people are excited to know that you're coming back to the land of the living."

He watched as she bustled about, taking away a water glass that was here, opening up the curtains. "Where am I?" he asked, an inane distrustfulness taking over his mind.

She smiled. "You're in an apartment," she noted. "And I'm Nancy, a private nurse hired to look after you."

"Thank you."

She laughed. "Don't thank me, thank your friends who brought me on board. Honestly I'm not even sure how or why you're awake right now, but I'm grateful that you are."

"Meaning?"

"Meaning, we weren't sure you would ever come back," she stated. "It's been touch-and-go for a while."

He felt the shock of her words hit his brain, but it wasn't making any sense. "Have my friends been here?"

"The one, yes," she confirmed easily. "Terk's been here many times."

"And, for that, I'm very grateful," Scott said. "I'm assuming he's the one who hired you?"

She nodded. "Absolutely. He's been very worried about you."

"Is there a way to contact him? Is there a phone I can use?" Just knowing Terk was alive and well made some of Scott's panic ease back. He needed answers, and that's something he knew Terk would have.

"I'll let him know that you're awake," she replied comfortably. "What I need you to do is stay in bed, relax, and, if you can sleep some more, do so. Now that you've surfaced, you'll find that your recovery is not quite as fast as you want it to be. Thus you'll need more rest than you expect."

He didn't say anything because, as far as he was concerned, nothing would be fast enough, and the last thing he expected to have was more time in bed. From the look on her face, she understood that's how it would be too.

He smiled. "I'll try," he noted, offering a compromise.

She laughed at that. "I've seen plenty of men like you," she confirmed. "I'll be grateful if you at least try, and I know full well that your attempt to be as quiet as what I would hope for will fail."

He shrugged. Disappointed, he lay quiet for a moment. What he had avoided doing was testing his muscles. He also hadn't asked her very many details on how long he'd been down and all. This would be a challenge to not get more data. He could only hope that he was in way better shape than he appeared already. Still, regardless of his injuries, he wanted information on his team. But that could bring on way more pain.

After she closed the door, he pushed back the blankets and stretched his legs, relieved to see that they were both there and that they could move freely. And then he slowly sat up. He stretched, rolled his neck and back, wondering what had happened because he seriously felt like he'd been hit by something heavy, maybe even a train, and he was only partially joking.

He sent out a message to his team, only to have it rebound right back. He frowned at that. They'd become accustomed to using their abilities to stay together as a unit, and so Scott couldn't understand when it returned, almost as if it were unanswerable. Not the kind of response he wanted. And it terrified him that there might not be anyone there to receive his message.

He tried again, but that message also came back. He frowned at that, hoping that his nurse would come back, with a phone that he could use.

Very gingerly, he stood and carefully made his way to the small adjoining room, hoping it was a bathroom. It was; with relief, he used the facilities. He wasn't even sure how any of this worked because, although he felt decent, and he couldn't see any injuries, his limbs felt like they were full of lead, and every movement was filled with pain. That surprised him. He thought he was in much better shape than this, especially after apparently having done nothing but slept for as long as he had. And what the hell had happened to drop him so hard?

When he walked out of the bathroom, Nurse Nancy stood there, glaring at him. He threw up his hands. "What? I'm not allowed to go to the bathroom?"

"Well, I guess, especially considering that I took your catheter out yesterday. On Terk's orders by the way," she noted.

He stared at her. "Terk told you to?"

She nodded. "Believe me. I wasn't sure about doing it, but he insisted that you were waking up. Interesting, since he wasn't even here at the time."

He smiled at her. "Yeah, Terk is like that."

"He's freaky," she muttered. "It went against everything in my training to follow his instructions, but he wouldn't listen to my advice."

"Well, he's the boss, I presume?"

"Yes, but not for much longer, apparently." She suspiciously studied Scott.

"Hey, it's all right," he murmured. "I have a history of doing really well, once I'm back on my feet."

"Maybe so," she admitted, "but don't kid yourself. Your system went through a lot. It's not healthy, and it's not doing as well as you or Terk might like it to be. You are definitely not in any shape to be dancing around and to be causing trouble."

He winced. "Wasn't planning on dancing for quite a while." He sank onto the bed. "And trouble has a way of finding me. Did you happen to get a phone?"

"I have mine," she noted. "I sent a message and told Terk that you were awake."

"And, for that, I thank you." He was elated to know that there was at least one phone.

"We'll see," she said. "As far as I'm concerned, you need to be in bed for another week."

At that, he raised one eyebrow and, in a deliberately mild voice, stated, "You'll have to adjust your expectations then because that'll never happen."

She glared at him and then shrugged irritably. "What is it about all you strong guys?" she asked. "It's like you're all against spending time in bed. You don't know how much I would love an opportunity to lay around and to relax in bed for a week."

With half a smile, he looked at her. "I like to stay in bed if I'm not alone, but it's another thing entirely to stay in bed because somebody considers me an invalid."

She laughed. "You're obviously healing if you're thinking along those lines." She gave a shake of her head.

"I'd like to be, yes." He glanced around his room. "I understand that you've been looking after me, and I really appreciate that, Nancy, but what are the chances of getting some food?"

She stopped, stared. "I'm not sure your stomach is quite ready for that."

"Unless you are willing to put the feeding tube and the IVs back in," he argued, holding out his arm, "I'll need food." He noted that only now did she realize he'd pulled out all his remaining tubes.

"Good Lord." She bustled forward. "You're just determined to be in charge, aren't you?" She shook her head. "Life would move along much easier for you if you would at least give your body a chance to recover."

"It's had way too long already," Scott stated. "And that's about as much as it'll get."

She sighed. "Nothing in life is quite that simple."

"No, it isn't, but you can bet that I want to be out and on my own," he stated. "I'll do as much as I can, as fast as I can. You never know when I'll need my abilities again." At the term, he winced because she was staring at him, clearly puzzled. He shrugged. "I was respected in my field," he added, "so it'll be hard to have people see me as not measuring up."

"Get used to it," she replied. "Everybody has that to overcome. We all have periods when we are in our prime, but too soon thereafter somebody else comes along, better and stronger than we are."

"Maybe," he admitted, "but some of us are still in our prime."

She smiled. "Don't worry. I'm not trying to knock you down or to tell you that you're anything less," she explained. "I can already tell you're ready to go. Let me go see what I can rustle up to eat. Chances are, if I don't feed you, I'll come back and find you gone, out looking for food on your own."

"Oh, I can cook," he noted.

At the doorway she stopped and glared at him. "Young man, you put your butt back in that bed," she ordered. "Otherwise I'll go lock up the kitchen, and you're not getting anything. Terk may be my boss, but you are not. So follow my instructions while you're here, or we'll have a problem." And, with that, she disappeared.

He stared at her retreating figure in surprise, and then he chuckled. It figured that Terk would find somebody like her to look after him. He had a healthy respect for women of all ages and occupations, but some were exceptional. And she appeared to be one of them. He settled back into bed smiling, only to lose his smile when he realized his body was sagging with relief.

He shouldn't be that tired. He shouldn't be that worn out. Not just from walking to the bathroom and back. It was the first indication he'd had that whatever happened to him had been bad and that he was far from being free and clear from whatever this nightmare was. He sat back in the bed to relax, hoping she brought lots of food when she returned to his room. Aside from the pain he felt, he had a ravenous hunger building that threatened to take over everything in his world right now. He hoped she would hurry up. Even as he thought about it, his stomach rumbled loudly.

And he settled back to wait.

NAIRA SAT ON the edge of her bed in her hotel room. Was there ever anything as quiet and unfriendly as a sterile hotel room? She'd gone to see Scott, and the visit had been harder than she'd expected. Normally she would have considered herself a very strong woman, able to handle stress like many people couldn't. But seeing Scott, with all the tubes running in and out of his system, his body slack, his eyes closed, looking almost dead, had been more than she could handle. And seeing her own reaction had been devastating because she thought she could do so much better, so as not to show Scott how scared she was.

Instead it had taken everything she had not to burst into tears and collapse beside him. Yet Terk had seemed to understand.

He'd led her away and stated calmly, "I know you don't want to believe me, but he is doing much better now."

She shook her head. "That's better?" she asked incredulously. "You're right. I don't believe you."

"Well, whatever you've been doing," Terk said, "has helped."

She stared at him in shock. "I haven't been doing anything," she cried out.

He smiled. "Yes, you have. And I've noticed."

She shook her head, yet again in confusion. "All I've done is pray," she murmured. "I prayed from the time you told me that he was in trouble, how maybe somebody would help him."

"Definitely people are helping him," Terk confirmed quietly. "That's a given. He is well loved."

She smiled. "That's good. He's a good man."

"Which is also why you're here," he noted.

"And I don't know why," she admitted, feeling bewildered. "When you called me, I didn't even know who you were."

"And you haven't kept in touch with Scott all this time, have you?"

"No. After I got married, it was just more than anybody could handle," she murmured.

"Does that seem out of line for him to not be in touch with you?"

"He's always been strong, and he never really showed any emotions, so I wasn't even sure how he felt when I told him that I was getting married."

"I'm sure he did his best to hide his reaction, needing to keep it under wraps," Terk explained. "I know the news devastated him."

"No, you're wrong," she argued. "I don't think he was affected at all."

"Because he didn't show it?" he asked her, with half a smile.

She nodded. "That, and it was just the way he acted. Completely nonchalant, as if he didn't care at all."

"And you believed him?"

"Of course I believed him," she replied. "But it didn't matter because I was already heading into a completely different stage of life."

"And I get that," Terk noted, "although I'm not sure what your relationship with Scott was like, yet obviously it wasn't that close."

"He was everything to me," she whispered. "Absolutely everything. Then we had a fight, and we never quite seemed to recover from it," she murmured, staring off in the distance. "And now, well, I'm not even sure what the fight was about."

"Yet you came when you found out he was injured."

"Of course I did," she snapped, bristling. "And I would again. He was an important part of my life, and, if nothing else, he's a solid human being. So, if I can do anything to help, I'm quite happy to."

"I'm glad to hear that," Terk said. "How do you feel about sticking around for a little while?"

She shook her head, looking confused. "Why would I do that?"

"Because he might need a friend when he wakes up."

"Is anybody but you saying he'll wake up?" she asked, staring at Terk. "I've got to tell you. Scott didn't look like he was anywhere close to joining the living."

"He's definitely still living," Terk stated, "but I can see how some doubts could be in your mind. I also know that he cared a lot for you."

"Yeah, in the past tense," she agreed.

"Did he ever mention anything recently about coming to see you?"

"No, not at all," she said. "I haven't had any contact with him, since I told him that I was getting married."

"Maybe that's to be expected," Terk noted.

"I don't know why," she stated. "Lots of people stay friends after they split."

"Sure, usually when they don't care as much as they used to," Terk added.

"Meaning?"

"I'm pretty sure Scott cares about you in a big way," Terk replied calmly. "And your news pretty well devastated him."

She laughed bitterly. "I don't know what your game is, and here I thought you knew him. But the truth of the matter is, everything you're saying right now sounds like a complete fabrication. If Scott cared, he never would have let me go ahead with it and get married."

"I don't think he felt like it was something for him to interfere in," Terk said, studying her carefully.

"Interesting that you'd phrase it that way."

"Did you get engaged, hoping Scott would stop it?"

She stared at him. "No, … not at all. I didn't say that."

"No, but you implied something along those lines that, if he really cared, he would have stopped it."

"Sure," she noted, "but he didn't care. He didn't say anything."

"But you'd already made a decision, hadn't you?"

"Yes," she replied, "but he also knew why."

"Why?" Obviously Terk was confused.

"It was a marriage of companies. A business arrangement," she stated, with an eye roll.

"For you?"

"My father, and he was pretty adamant that I follow through."

"So you did."

"I did, and, yes, I regretted it from the moment I agreed, but, once I had, the ball was rolling, and I could really do nothing to stop it. At least not easily."

"Did your father know that you already cared about somebody else?"

"Yes, but he wouldn't have anything to do with Scott. Never did, never would. It was obvious that, for peace in the family, I needed to do this. If Scott cared, he would have tried to talk me out of it at least, but he just told me that, since I had made a decision, he would stand by it."

"Of course he did," Terk noted. "What else could he do?"

"Well, it would have been nice if he'd swept me up and taken me away to a new world," she admitted bitterly.

Terk frowned. "I'm sorry, but were you really expecting that?"

"No," she snapped. "I wasn't expecting anything, and basically I got what I expected, which was complete indifference. He didn't care what happened, so I got married." She shrugged.

"Really? That is a strange way of putting it," he murmured.

"Not if it's a business arrangement," she argued. "That happens way more than you want to believe. I'm not sure I even believe in happily ever after."

At that, Terk laughed. "Now you sound like me."

She shook her head free of that past conversation. Now here she sat, waiting. Waiting for what though? Going over old memories? First, she should stop rehashing all that nonsense in the past. And, second, she could do this at home more easily than here. She sighed, wondering at her sanity right now.

She stared at the walls of the hotel room around her, questioning what she was even doing here. It's not as if Scott would be happy to see her, and now that she'd seen Scott in the hospital, then later in a special apartment set up for him, she didn't know what she was supposed to do. When the phone rang, it startled her. Taking a deep breath, she answered, stunned to find it was Terk, as if he had heard her jumbled thoughts and was calling in response.

"He just woke up," Terk announced, and such joy filled his voice that she smiled.

"I'm glad," she said. "Now he should be okay, right?"

"In theory, yes," he replied gently. "I want to pick you up, so we can see him."

"No. That's not a good idea. I came to make sure he was okay. Now that I know he is, there's no point in my staying." An odd sound of surprise came on the other end of the phone, but she shook her head. "I still don't know what it is that you think is supposed to happen here," she admitted, "but it's obviously not something that I really want to be a part of."

"What is it that you think is happening?" Terk asked curiously.

She frowned. "I don't know, but it feels like it's none of my concern."

"Not for me," he replied instantly. "My concern is keeping Scott alive."

"But now he's awake—and knowing him—he's probably stronger than ever. It seems like, every time he falls, he bounces back even better."

At that, Terk laughed. "You do understand him."

"Maybe. I also understand that he won't be happy to see me."

"I think you're wrong, Naira," Terk argued. "And just because he's there, and you're afraid to go meet him, doesn't mean that you should give in to that fear."

She gasped in outrage. "I've done everything you asked," she snapped. "And now that it's obvious he'll be okay, since he's awake, you certainly don't need me anymore."

"Maybe I don't, but what if Scott needs you?" And after a few seconds of silence, Terk added, "I'll be there in a few minutes." With that, he rang off.

She stared down at the phone in her hands, wondering at the foolishness that had brought her here. It had made so much sense when it happened initially because all she could think about was Scott and keeping him alive. She didn't even know why she had been such an easy target, but it felt like she had been in some way. It was a very strange feeling.

A knock came on her door. When it opened, before she'd even had a chance to get there, she stared at Terk in surprise. "I didn't even open the door," she protested.

He nodded. "I wouldn't give you a chance to say no."

She glared at him. "That's hardly fair."

"Nothing's fair in love and war," he murmured. "And, right now, this is all about love."

"Maybe it was about love once," she admitted, with a shake of her head, "but it hasn't been for a very long time."

"I think you're wrong," Terk stated. "But regardless you need to come, so we can go see him."

"I disagree. And this isn't what I want to do."

"So, what do you want to do?" Terk asked, his hands on his hips as he stared at her. "Are you prepared to walk through life without seeing him again?" She frowned because she hadn't really thought about that. Yet, even as the thought penetrated her foggy, confused brain, her heart was screaming. She shrugged. "Maybe," she replied, but it was a weak effort at that, and she knew Terk understood it too.

"Come on," Terk said in a voice that she found herself automatically obeying. And how the hell did that work? "Let's go see him."

"And how do you even know he's awake?"

"His nurse contacted me," he murmured. "He's confused, a little upset, and he doesn't know the full extent of what happened to his team or what happened to him."

"Well, it sounds like you're the one who needs to go, so you can fill him in on those details," she noted, with a shrug. "It's got nothing to do with me."

"It has a lot to do with you," he murmured. "And he's asking about you."

She stopped and stared. "What?" she asked, shaking her head in disbelief. "What do you mean, he asked about me? He doesn't even know I was there."

"Well, that's one of the reasons I think it's important that you come," Terk explained, "because he seems to remember that you were there."

She shook her head. "That's not possible. He was in a coma. Remember? You and I both know he was. He can't possibly have a clue that I was there."

"Scott asked the nurse about it. He believes you were there, and he's confused. Is that how you want to leave him?"

She frowned, and of course the answer was no. "I feel so—" Then she stopped.

"Yes?" Terk asked helpfully. She turned and glared at him, saying nothing. After a few awkward moments, he broke the silence. "Confused? Irritated? Upset? Anxious? Uncertain? All of the above?" he asked, with a smile on his face.

She nodded slowly. "Yes, that's part of it," she murmured. "It's not that easy, you know?"

"Nothing about relationships is easy," Terk confirmed.

"Are you married?"

Immediately the smile faded from his face, and he shook his head. "No. I'm not."

"Well, if at any time you do decide to go in that direction," she murmured, "you might want to wipe that smug smile off your face because most women won't appreciate it." And, with that, she preceded him out the door.

CHAPTER 2

T HE WHOLE TRIP there, Naira fidgeted. Yet Terk never said a word. He just calmly drove back to where Scott was. She frowned. "You know, once he's awake, he'll just get up and bolt back to life again."

"Of course," Terk agreed. "His whole team is like that."

"Of course they are," she said, with an eye roll. "This whole big-strong-male thing really gets old. You know that, right?"

He chuckled. "We are who we are," he murmured. "And, for one reason or another, you two were friends."

"More than friends," she murmured, as she stared out the passenger window. "It seems like a long time ago."

"And maybe it's time for second chances," he murmured.

She shook her head. "That'll never happen." Terk didn't say anything, but she almost heard that never-say-never refrain going through the vehicle. Thankfully they arrived sooner than she expected. She frowned, not at all ready for this. "I thought we were farther away."

"No, Scott's right here." They hopped out, and she followed him inside the apartment. It seemed different.

"It even seems like another apartment."

"We're coming in from a second entrance," he murmured.

She shrugged, not sure what to say, but almost immediately they reached an apartment door that opened under his knock. She smiled at the same nurse she'd seen before. "Is he really awake?" Naira asked.

The nurse nodded and beamed. "He is, indeed." She looked over at Terk. "You were right. Good thing I didn't bet on it."

"Maybe so," Terk noted, with a smile.

She snorted. "Somehow I don't think you're wrong very often."

"Just enough to keep me humble," he murmured.

The nurse stared at him. "I'm not sure *humble* and *you* go together in the same sentence," she teased.

And Naira had to agree. Something was very assertive about Terk. It wasn't that he had an arrogance to him but definitely an odd sense of power or authority that she didn't recognize.

The nurse led the way into the kitchen, and Naira immediately saw Scott. He was sitting up normally, as if nothing had happened, working his way through a stack of pancakes. He looked up and blinked. And then he blinked again.

Stunned, she shook her head. "Good God," she murmured. "When I saw you just yesterday, I could have sworn that you would never wake up again."

He swallowed the pancakes, looked over at Terk, then back at her. "I thought I saw you," he replied, disbelief in his voice.

"How is it that you saw me?" she murmured, staring at him in fascination. "You were in a coma."

He nodded. "I was, but I was also very aware of what was going on around me."

She shook her head, more than a little disturbed by that concept. "That's not normal," she declared.

Scott just smiled, as Terk laughed. "Remember now. Nothing's normal about any of us."

At that, the nurse nodded. "That's for sure. Since Scott woke up, he's done nothing but eat," she noted, looking at Terk, with an accusingly stare.

Terk nodded. "And I warned you about that, didn't I?"

She glared at him. "Well, there's eating, and then there's eating. That's his third stack of pancakes."

Terk assessed the food in front of Scott, then shrugged. "He hasn't eaten for weeks and weeks," he noted, "so I can see him trying to fill back up again."

The nurse stared at him and frowned. "There's no place for it."

"He's empty, that's all," Terk added. "He's fine. He'll eat until his body tells him to stop." Just then it appeared that his body had spoken because, even as Naira watched, Scott put down his fork and looked as if he were suddenly ready to bolt.

Terk walked over and placed a hand on his friend's shoulder. "It's good to see you up."

Naira watched, as if somehow a message passed between them, and Scott settled back at the table.

"It's good to be back," Scott murmured, then stared up at Terk. "We have a lot to discuss."

"We do," Terk agreed, "but not today. You still have a lot to adapt to, and your brain isn't fully functioning."

At that, he snorted. "My brain is always functioning."

"You might think so," Terk replied, "but you have an awful lot of information to assimilate."

Naira took a deep breath and sat down at the table. She

could be an adult about this. The decision to be here had come from her heart, and it was really good to see that Scott was doing so well, compared to what she'd seen yesterday. With that, she smiled at him. "I'm really glad you pulled through this," she said, as she reached across and touched his fingers. "Terk called me," she murmured. "Otherwise I wouldn't have known." He just gave her a flat stare, and, after a moment, she shrugged. "So you can be as unhappy as you want to be that I'm here, but, if you want to be pissed about it, you can be pissed at Terk, okay?" And, with that, she cheerfully threw Terk under the bus.

Terk snorted. "And it worked, didn't it?" he murmured.

She stared at him. "Says you."

"What worked?" Scott asked.

"You weren't showing enough progress," Terk explained calmly. "So I needed to pull in the heavy guns."

"Naira's the heavy guns?" Scott asked, with an odd tone.

Terk just smiled a mysterious smile that made everybody stare at him. "It worked, so I'll say yes."

Naira looked over at the man who was studiously avoiding her. "This is hardly the time to talk," she noted, "but I certainly don't regret coming over and seeing you. When I found out what had happened," she said, with a head shake, "I was pretty stunned."

"Well, you know more than I do," he stated, "because I don't even know what happened."

"And you won't for another day or so," Terk replied.

"Do you really think a day will make any difference?"

"Well, yesterday you were unconscious, so, yes."

Scott glared at him.

"You're not quite up to snuff yet."

"The hell I'm not," Scott argued.

"You're not," Terk replied in a tone that brooked no arguments.

Scott nodded slowly. "I'll give you one day. After that, ... I'll get filled in one way or another," he replied, his tone hard.

Terk nodded. "We'll see."

Scott shook his head. "No," he muttered. "No more games."

At that, Terk gave him a hard stare. "I don't think anything I've done would be considered a game by any measure," he muttered.

Scott winced at that. "I hope not because that would really piss me off."

"I'm doing what I'm doing because I believe it's the right thing to do. If you don't like it, you know what you can do about it," Terk added, his tone soft but measured.

And, of course, Scott did know.

At least Naira assumed so because he immediately turned in his chair, then looked at the pancakes and picked up his fork and started eating again.

She shook her head. "Wow, I don't think I've ever seen you eat like this before." At that, he just gave her a look, and she almost smiled at him. "Yeah, I get it," she replied cheerfully. "You're not happy I'm here. Deal with it, okay? Because I am."

He ignored her completely and kept on eating.

She looked over at Terk. "So, do I get to go home now?"

Scott immediately answered. "Hell yes."

Terk shook his head. "Nope."

"I'm hardly your prisoner," Naira snapped, glaring at Terk.

"No, you're not," Terk agreed, "but Scott still needs

you."

At that, Scott looked at him in shock. "What the hell are you talking about? I haven't had anything to do with her in a very long time."

"Yeah, I hear you," Terk noted quietly. "But, when push came to shove, she's the one who came, and immediately you healed."

"It was probably just shock," he said, almost belligerently.

"I don't care what it was," Terk murmured. "I would do a lot to keep my friends alive and well—even if they're not happy about it."

"You'll just have to make some adjustments then, won't you?" Scott snapped.

And, with that, Terk headed toward the main room. "I have to talk to the nurse."

"Yeah, and you can figure out how to pay her off so she can leave, and you can spring me free from this apartment," he murmured.

"Yeah, I'll do that, whenever I decide that you're well enough to be free." And he walked out, leaving Scott still glaring at Terk.

"Boy, he really does know how to get your goat, doesn't he?" Naira murmured, with a smile.

He shrugged. "As he said, he does it because he cares."

"Oh, I get that," she murmured. "He really does care, and you're blessed to have him."

"Maybe," Scott said, "but there are days though …"

At that, she grinned. "Absolutely." She eyed him critically. "Honestly I get why he's saying what he's saying, but you do look pretty decent for somebody who wouldn't survive."

"And who said I wouldn't survive?" he snapped.

"I wouldn't have put it past you to live against all the odds," she admitted; then he got quiet. "Honestly it was pretty rough seeing you like that. It was awful."

He had the grace to look ashamed at that point. "I'm sorry if you made the trip for nothing," he murmured.

"It wasn't for nothing," she argued. "Besides, I was happy to see you again."

"Why's that?" he asked. And then he frowned. "Unless of course you're divorced again."

"Again?" She tried to hide the hurt in her voice. "It's hardly like I've been divorced before."

"No. … That was uncalled for. I'm sorry." He took a deep breath and rubbed his face with both hands. "I appear to be a little off balance right now."

"That's one word for it." She stared at him for a long moment and then nodded. "And you're right. I am divorced. But there's no *again* about it. It was just the one marriage."

"It was still one marriage," he noted, with casual indifference.

"Like you're so perfect?"

"No, absolutely not perfect at all," he admitted, shaking his head. "But I sure as hell won't marry someone I don't give a shit about."

"No," she agreed, "you just don't give a shit about anybody."

SCOTT WASN'T SURE what the hell was going on in his world, but having Naira here, having her this close, was painful, which, after all this time, was so damn wrong. He didn't want to admit it, and he didn't want anything to do with it at all, but he'd been thrown off balance by everything since he woke up.

The fact that Terk also hadn't filled Scott in on what had happened to him was frustrating. It seemed like every time he turned around, he had something else to adjust to, and his powers of adjustment were definitely lacking. Terk was right about that. As usual. So Scott needed a day to assimilate everything that had gone on. He'd give himself that day, but he'd be damned if he'd give himself any more than that. He wasn't raised to be namby-pamby, and, when there was shit to deal with, he would be there one way or another.

He didn't have a clue what to even say to Naira. The fact that she was here and had come because he was injured said a lot, but it was a hard thing for him to even swallow. She had gotten married, and he'd tried hard to walk away and to let her make her own wrong choices, but it had been hard. It had been damn hard. The fact that she had seemed to make this decision to marry so casually had also bothered him.

To him, marriage was a contract, but it was a sacred one. Something that you honored and stuck to. He knew divorce happened, and sometimes it should, but he didn't want to be one of the many cases contributing to the statistics, like so many others out there. And, when she had been so casual about her marriage to somebody else, it had been all he could do to not scream foul. He thought he and Naira were going somewhere. Maybe he'd been taking too long to get there, and she could probably be justified in feeling pissed off at him for that, but to turn around and marry somebody else?

Hell no, that's not the way he rolled. Obviously it's the way she did, and that was fine, as long as it didn't have anything to do with him. She could play her own games. The fact that she was here now bothered him because he needed to recover, not be constantly off balance. She was the one sending him off balance, and that was hard. He wanted Naira and the nurse gone. It didn't seem like they would leave anytime soon, and that didn't help him either. He finished the plate in front of him, then sat back, and he felt the fatigue hitting him. He might have tanked up a little bit too much, and his body would need recuperation time now.

Terk walked in just then.

"I'll have to crash."

Terk immediately nodded. "We'll see you when you wake up."

"You will." Then he looked over at Naira. "Thanks for coming," he stated formally. "It's obvious that I'm doing much better now, so I'm sure you'll be happy to go back to your world." And, with that, he got up and stumbled to his room. As soon as he was inside, with the door shut, he crashed on the bed and tried hard to forget the look of hurt on her face.

What was he supposed to do? Welcome her with open arms or something? After all he'd been through? Hell no. He knew perfectly well that this was a dangerous time, and he had to recover, but that didn't mean that he had to open himself up to all kinds of emotional pain from his past. That was just asking for more problems.

He didn't have the time, patience, or tolerance for it either. If she wanted something from him, she had picked the wrong time because he needed to focus on giving himself the best chance he could, in order to recover from this. And just nothing was going smoothly right now. He needed time, and he had one day; that was it. Then he would be hell-bent for leather, getting out of here and figuring out what was going on.

And, with that, he closed his eyes and crashed.

CHAPTER 3

Once Naira got into the vehicle, she told Terk, "I'm booking my flight to go home. Thank you for all you've done for him."

"Well, you're not leaving," Terk noted calmly, "so you might as well not bother."

"I am definitely leaving," she snapped, glaring at him. "It's not like you can stop me. There are laws about such things, you know?"

"Sure there are," Terk agreed, "but you also know that what you saw today was just a reaction on his part. A reaction to pain. The shock of seeing you and the shock of realizing how much his own life had changed. Yet he doesn't even know what happened to him yet, much less the rest of the team."

"Sure, and another day from now," she replied, "you'll fill him all in, and he'll have forgotten I was ever there."

"Only if you let him," Terk argued, looking at her with a hard expression. "Is that what you want?"

She raised both hands in frustration, as she unconsciously moved as close to the passenger door as she could get. "What is it that you want from me?" she snapped. "You told me that he was injured, and I came running. Now what? He doesn't want anything to do with me. That's obvious. He told me to leave in no uncertain terms."

"And it's also obvious that he didn't mean it," Terk added. "He reacted blindly, back to his old habit, because that's how he knows to react to you. Your circumstances have changed, and so have his."

She shook her head. "He hasn't changed a bit," she said, trying hard to keep the bitterness out of her tone. "He's just as difficult as always."

At that, Terk looked at her. "Did you really think he would have changed?"

"I don't know," she replied. "I guess I'd hoped so."

Terk shook his head. "Change happens, but it can take a bit of time to assimilate."

"Well, he doesn't want any time with me," she murmured. "So you can forget all about that."

"I'm not trying to matchmake here," he stated. "So you can do you, but his health is what I'm concerned about."

She looked at him. "I don't get it. It's obvious that he's doing really well."

"He is, and yet he isn't," Terk murmured. "You know perfectly well that a lot of the reason Scott's even alive right now is you."

Shaking her head, she frowned. "I don't know what you're talking about."

He groaned. "You know what? It would be really nice if people weren't always so dumb in spirit."

"And it would be really nice if people like you weren't always so full of themselves," she snapped. "You're not even making sense."

"It's your prayers, Naira," Terk explained. "It's you calling to him that brought him back out of that terrible state he was in."

She shook her head. "That's just wishful thinking on

your part," she murmured, "though I don't even know why you would want it to be that way."

He sighed. "I'll drop you off at your hotel to think about it. Then you can call me when you're ready to talk."

"And again you're not listening to me. There's nothing to say."

"There's a lot to say. That's why I want you to go think about it."

"I'm not a child," she snapped.

He looked at her, frowned, and replied, "Honestly it would be a lot easier if you were. Then it wouldn't be quite so difficult to get people to do what they needed to do."

"You mean, what *you* say people need to do," she said, a harsh snap to her voice.

"Exactly." He nodded. "I'm glad you're finally getting that."

"Just because you say this is what needs to happen doesn't mean it is." The gall of the man …

"It absolutely is," Terk disagreed. "So stop trying to be difficult and please let's just keep Scott alive."

The *keep Scott alive* part stunned her. And, when she slammed the door closed and watched as Terk drove off, she wondered just how serious he was.

She took three steps toward the front of the hotel, then felt a pull on her shoulder, before she ever heard a sound— the grinding of brakes as Terk stopped abruptly and backed up. Then she heard other people crying out. She looked around, bewildered, suddenly aware of this pain in her arm, in her shoulder, and an icy coldness. Terk bolted from the car and ran to her. She looked up at him and slowly moved into his arms. "I don't feel so good," she whispered.

"No," he said, "I get that. Not to worry, we'll take care

of you."

But she could tell that he was worried that something more serious was wrong. She shook her head. "Somehow I don't think there's anything you can do." Then she sagged against him. She heard people yelling and the sound of people running. She looked up at him. "What just happened?" she whispered.

He held her close. "You were shot," he told her gently. "Just stay relaxed. Help is on the way." At the term *shot*, she froze, and suddenly everything—the pain, shock, and fear—bombarded her, and she collapsed, unconscious.

SCOTT JERKED AWAKE when the phone that Terk had left suddenly rang. Scott noted it was Terk. With a snort, Scott answered it. "What the hell?" he asked. "Don't I get any peace now?"

"Probably not," Terk replied. "Naira was just shot outside her hotel."

Scott cried out, with a sound he would never have imagined coming from his throat. "What happened?" he asked, bolting to his feet, looking around for his clothes.

"I had just dropped her off, and she was planning on booking a flight out, although I had asked her to stay and to think it over," Terk explained. "But she was adamant that she was leaving, that you didn't want anything to do with her, and that it had not been a mistake to come, but she wouldn't compound it by staying."

"Shit," Scott murmured.

"Yeah, that's one word for it," Terk agreed. "I'm at the hospital right now."

"I'll be there in five minutes."

"No, you won't," Terk stated in a warning voice. "I can't have two of you to look after."

"Well, that's just too damn bad," Scott snapped in a harsh voice. "This is all my fault."

"Yeah, and how do you figure that?" Terk asked, with interest in his voice. "Did you shoot her?"

"Of course I didn't fucking shoot her," he roared into the phone, as he grabbed his clothes.

"Then stop trying to take blame for something that isn't yours."

"Who the hell did this?" he asked, stopping to stare at his phone.

"The same group that we've been after for the last couple weeks, I'm sure."

"A couple weeks? Why the hell haven't you solved this?" he asked.

"Because we were operating without much in the way of a team. Almost nobody is truly back up to full speed yet. Everybody had to come back up slowly," Terk added, "and you're no different."

"Hell if I'm not," he snapped. "I've never done anything slowly in my life." And, with that, he hung up. He walked out to find the nurse, sitting there, playing a card game of solitaire. "I have to go to the hospital."

She bolted to her feet. "What's the matter?" Nancy asked, rushing over to him, looking to see what was wrong.

He shook his head. "Not me, the woman who was just here," he replied.

"What about her?" she asked in confusion.

"She was shot. I have to go."

"No, no, no," she cried out. "That's not a good idea."

"Well, if I collapse again," he noted, with a touch of humor, "at least I'll be in the right place. Call me a cab." She immediately shook her head, and he shrugged, pulled out his phone, and instead ordered an Uber. "I'm leaving. I will be back, hopefully soon. I don't know," he explained. "It depends on how badly Naira's hurt."

"Yet you don't care," she stated, an intent look at his face. "And it's obvious, since you sent her away."

"Oh, thanks." He glared at her. "That's really not what I want to be reminded of, especially while she's possibly dying at the hospital."

She nodded. "I understand that, but you need to get your head on straight before you go flying in there. You can't add to her stress or to her pain either."

He took a deep breath because, of course, Nancy was right. "I'll be fine, once I get there."

"You'll be fine when you figure out that she's alive and well, but not so fine until then?" she snapped. "So don't go thinking that the rest of us don't know what you're talking about."

He glared, but there was no arguing with Nancy because she was right. "I still need to get to the hospital."

"Have at it. I would have called the cab for you if you'd listened to what I had to say for two minutes," she stated.

He groaned, realizing he was alienating everybody who had been there for him. "I'm not trying to be a jerk," he murmured, "but I can't leave her at the hospital."

"So what will you do?" she asked, giving him a hard flat stare. "It's not as if you can pull her out of there, and that's exactly where she needs to be right now. Hopefully Terk got her there right away, so she can get the best care."

"She will," he noted. Sitting down suddenly at the kitchen table, he scrubbed his face with both hands. "I don't know what I'll do if something happens to her."

"Well, you'll start with forgiving yourself," the nurse stated, her voice calmer than before.

He shook his head. "No, I need her alive so I can apologize."

"And that's just selfishness on your part." She gave him another one of those looks. "Maybe think about her for a moment."

He looked at the nurse, stunned, and she nodded.

"Obviously there are hard feelings between the two of you," she explained, "but just think about what it would have taken for her to come all the way over here, then seeing you looking so bad and suddenly better, only to be treated to the reception that you gave her, not to mention the demand that she leave."

He winced. "Fine, I'm an ass. I get it, but, at the same time, I've just come out of a deep coma myself, and I'm not exactly sure where my head's at."

"Your head is nowhere," she agreed. "Why do you think Terk wanted you to spend the day getting back onto your feet? You need more than even that, of course, but obviously he knows you well and realizes that no way you would give him longer than that."

Scott stared at her for a long moment. "Do you know anything about what happened to her?"

"No," the nurse replied. "Terk hasn't contacted me."

"I'm still going."

"Of course you are, but maybe you won't go with so much vengeance in your heart."

He winced. "Is that what it looks like?"

Her voice was gentle as she answered, "Listen. It's obvious that you care for Naira, whether you want to admit it or not, and, if she had a chance to see clearly, I'm sure she'd have noticed it herself."

"I'm not sure that's any better either," he murmured.

"Of course it is," Nancy said. "If people would just start to communicate, it would be a hell of a lot easier on relationships. When someone's older or when someone's shot, there's no time to waste on this BS. Get to the point or get out because there are not enough days in our lives to spend any of them sitting here and worrying ourselves into the grave over people who can't be bothered to find clarity in their own lives. If you want anything to do with her, or even if you don't," Nancy clarified, "you might want to consider at least finding a solution or coming to a place of peace over this whole thing for yourself."

Just then came a honk outside. She nodded at him. "Go, but make sure you get your ass back here soon, and, if you come back in any worse shape, it will be me you answer to."

With that, Scott disappeared.

CHAPTER 4

T HE NEXT MANY hours were a haze of pain and panic of
what seemed to be a never-ending stream of people into
her world. Naira surfaced a couple times to answer questions
and then gratefully sank back under again—only to be
dragged back up out of the depths with more questions. No,
she wasn't allergic to anything. No, she had no idea what
happened. No, she didn't see anybody. Yes, she had insurance. She always wondered about things like that.

Were there always so many questions? Didn't anybody
give a shit that she'd been shot, for God's sake? Surely there
were better things for people to be doing to help her other
than asking her these kinds of questions. But, from their
perspective, there wasn't anything better to do. That just
made her even sadder because what screwed-up world had
gotten them to this point? Nobody would be asking her all
that at such an inopportune time if it weren't required for
some reason. More evidence that the world was determined
to self-destruct. Thankfully, just when she started to think
she couldn't handle it anymore, she felt herself sliding back
under, and this time it stuck.

When she woke the next time, she looked around to find
herself in a room, apparently a private room at that. Dazed,
groggy, and not exactly sure what was going on, she drifted
under, popped back up, then drifted under again.

When she woke up the next time, she had a hell of a headache. She groaned as she surfaced, feeling the pain crushed against her skull, like somebody was beating it with a hammer.

Somebody immediately placed a gentle hand on her shoulder and whispered, "Take it easy. The nurse is here with pain meds."

She didn't even have to do anything before somebody jabbed her, and she was under yet again.

When she woke the next time, the pain still clawed at her, but it wasn't doing it with twenty-pound sledgehammers. She opened her eyes and saw another room, at least she thought it was another room. She wasn't exactly sure about that, but she noticed right away that she could breathe a bit easier. She took a slow deep breath, shuddered at the pain, then tried for shallower ones. Almost immediately another hand rested on her shoulder, followed by someone saying, "Take it easy now. You've been shot. The bullet punctured a lung, but you'll be fine. You need to stay calm though. And, yeah, breathing will hurt."

She opened her eyes, frowning to see through the pain, finding Scott smiling down on her. "What happened?" she asked again.

"You were shot after getting out of Terk's vehicle at the hotel," he murmured.

She stared up at him, as her brain tried to process the information. "Right. All that noise. People were everywhere."

"That's what happens when you get hurt," he said, once again with what almost sounded a bit like laughter in his voice.

"Don't like it," she muttered and shifted in the bed, only to cry out again.

"That's another thing that happens when you get hurt," he added. "Every movement you take is miserable."

She focused on her breathing, trying hard to stay calm through the mounds and shards of pain stabbing through her.

"I'll get the nurse for you," he said and immediately disappeared.

She didn't really want to see a nurse, but, at the same time, she didn't know what she needed or wanted. The pain was everywhere, all-encompassing and horrific, taking over the control of her mind. Only minutes later the pain medicine was added through her IV, and she crashed again. One of her last thoughts as she went under was confusion as to why Scott was still here.

When she woke again, she saw no sign of him, and she wondered if she had imagined his presence. She shifted on the bed gently, trying to reposition herself. She realized that her breathing was a little bit easier, and, although it still felt like she had been hit by a cement truck, it didn't feel like the cement truck was still sitting on her. She lay here, trying to focus on getting air into her lungs without it killing her.

The door opened, and Terk stepped inside; somehow he knew that she was awake. She watched him as he approached. "Good to see you awake," he said.

"If this is awake," she murmured, "I'm not sure it's a good place to be."

"No, I'm sure you don't." Terk smiled. "However, you are doing much better."

"If you say so," she muttered, and even then a shudder rippled up and down her body. He immediately reached over, and pulled the blankets higher up on her shoulders. She whispered, "I guess I'm not flying home today, huh?"

"No, not today, not tomorrow, and probably not for a few days with that lung injury," Terk explained. "They won't want you to fly for quite a while probably."

She felt hot tears in the corner of her eyes. "That's a shitty thing," she murmured.

"It is," he agreed, "and I'm very sorry that you got hurt."

She didn't know what to say to that. "You didn't shoot me," she murmured, "so it's not your fault."

"No, but I knew that getting you involved in this was a risk."

"But you were prepared to pay the price," she noted, trying hard to keep the pain from her voice, but knew she had failed. Then she realized it wasn't for her to care about just now. What difference did it make?

"No," Terk admitted, "you're right. I wasn't thinking about you. I was thinking about Scott."

And how could she argue with that? Tears whispered down her cheeks again. "Please tell him to go get some rest and to stop fussing over me. He needs to be looking after himself."

"He's leaving in just a few minutes," Terk told her. "He insisted on checking on you again before he goes."

"That's pretty stupid," she said. "He made it very clear that he didn't give a shit."

"I don't think he made *anything* very clear," Terk murmured. "And right now he probably has less clarity than before."

She didn't know what to say to that, so she said nothing.

When the door opened again, a nurse bustled in and shooed Terk out. "That's enough now. She needs to rest."

Grateful, Naira heard Terk walk out of the room, without saying another word. She thought he would at least say goodbye. Then she heard his voice in the room, saying goodbye. Yet he was no longer in the room.

She thought she had hallucinated, since the pain meds were kicking in. So it could just as easily have been his voice coming through the waves of pain battering through her system. It didn't matter because she was going under, and she hoped that, this time, she managed to stay there long enough that, when she woke again, the pain would be manageable. And, with that, she slipped back under.

OUTSIDE IN THE hallway, Scott looked at Terk. "And?"

"She was cognizant and talking a little bit," Terk replied. "The nurse increased the pain meds, and Naira's gone back under." He watched Scott hunch his shoulders.

"It's just really shitty," Scott muttered.

"It is, indeed," Terk confirmed. "Unfortunately it's also the reality of everything we're dealing with right now."

"And you still haven't gotten anywhere?"

"That's not really a fair assessment," Terk replied. "We've gotten somewhere several times, but unfortunately these people are killing off their own local hires, so, by the time we get anyone to talk to, to try and get some information from, they're pretty well taken out before we get a chance to do anything. We have talked to several to some degree, and, in each case," he murmured, "they haven't had any idea who it was they were in contact with, much less anyone higher up the ladder. A lot of dead bodies follow behind us right now," he explained. "MI6 is getting pretty pissed off at us."

"You think? It sounds like you're leaving them bodies to

deal with every time you turn around."

"We are, indeed," Terk said, cracking a smile. "But, in each case, these low-level hit men are not exactly high on England's wish list for new residents in their country."

"Not exactly citizens of the year, huh?"

"No, not at all," Terk murmured. "And that's about the only thing keeping MI6 even slightly patient with our investigation."

"I can see that," Scott admitted. He stretched gently, feeling the fatigue pull at him. He kept pulling on his reserves, trying hard to stay upright and with it enough that he could be of some value, but it was getting harder.

"You need to go get some rest," Terk stated, as usual noting Scott's energy levels.

"I keep trying to order myself to stay stronger," Scott murmured. "It works for a little bit, and then it crashes."

"It's only working," Terk noted in exasperation, "because I keep fortifying your energy levels. But the problem with that is, you're draining me at the same time, and I don't have too much more to give."

Scott looked over at Terk, startled. "Shit, and here I thought it was me."

"It's not. It's me. So I need you to go take care of your own energy levels," Terk said. "And that means, you're out of here."

Scott slowly nodded. "I forgot that you had the ability to direct all that energy to us."

"That's because I do it all the time," Terk noted. "However, now I'm still keeping Brody alive on the ethers too."

Scott stared at Terk in shock. "He's lost on the ethers?"

Terk nodded. "That's one word for it. Thankfully, Cara, a healer, found him."

"And she didn't help him?"

"She was focused and using all her energy on keeping Rick alive," Terk told Scott. "She didn't even know who Brody was and had no idea he had anything to do with us. Plus, you have to understand. She had one assignment, and an awful lot of people are out there floating. She has to stay focused."

"Jesus," Scott said, "we have to get Brody back."

"Oh, I agree. But, in order for that to happen, I need you to take care of yourself," Terk stated forcibly.

Scott winced. "Fine, but, if I go back there and try to sleep, you need to be tracking down whoever did this to Naira."

At that, Terk just looked at him, silent for a few moments. "Do you really think I'm not?"

"I know you are," Scott admitted in frustration. "Why can't I go back to the compound with the rest of you?"

"If I thought it was safe, I'd be all for it," Terk said. "But I'm not even going back there right now because I don't want to lead anybody from this nightmare to the rest of the team. They've got enough problems already. We are in communication with them though," he shared, "and they're all at work, tracking down Naira's shooter. The admins are following the traffic cams, and they're doing everything they can, working with MI6, not to mention Levi and Ice, trying to find out who the hell is behind this."

"I think the answer is still pretty damn easy," Scott stated. "I think it's our own government guys."

"And that may very well be," Terk noted. "The problem with it being our own guys is it doesn't look like they did this themselves."

At that, Scott stopped and looked at him in shock. "Are

you saying that you think they hired out the job?"

"Well, think about it," Terk explained. "If they did, and this is a contract, they would be removed from it."

"Sure, but contracts lead back to people."

"And yet everybody in the middle is dead," Terk added, "so who will dead guys lead back to?"

Scott winced at that. "God, what a mess."

"Exactly, so could you please go back and take care of yourself and build up some energy. Then we'll plan on getting you to the compound in a couple days."

"Will a couple days work?" he asked. "And who'll stand watch here on Naira?"

"Probably me," Terk admitted.

At that, Scott shook his head. "No, let me stay then. She came over here for me."

"Yes," Terk agreed, "but I pretty well forced her into it."

Scott just stared at his friend. "Why would you even think that was a good thing?"

"Because I could already tell, once I told her what had happened to you, that she would be sending you healing energy. And that healing energy is something you were desperately in need of. You also know it only comes from one source."

"We were close for a time," he admitted gruffly.

"In her mind, you're still close, but she thinks you didn't care enough to try to stop her from getting married. So she went through with it."

"Of course I cared, but what do you do when somebody you love comes to you and tells you that they're getting married as part of some idiotic business arrangement?"

"Obviously it's not by choice," Terk pointed out, "but I've always thought most relationships were beyond odd."

"Which is why you've avoided them," Scott stated.

At that, Terk went on, "Apparently I'll have to learn more about the matter. … You'll find out soon enough, so you might as well hear it from me." Then Terk told Scott about Celia.

"Good God." Scott stared at him. "You make all my problems look minor."

"That's not my intention, but it does make me more than a little worried. I need to get stateside as soon as we get the rest of this squared away."

"Did Ice say anything about how Celia's doing?"

"She's awake from her coma, but she has absolutely no recollection of what happened to her," Terk said.

"And how is that even possible?" Scott asked in bewilderment. "And she has to know you. I mean—" Scott slid a sideways glance at his friend. "I mean, it was your sperm, right?"

"Yes."

"You've checked?"

"No, I haven't. But I'm hardly likely to make a mistake on something like that."

Scott frowned. "But, with this so personal, you could be making a mistake, and it may be something that you need to look at."

"That would require testing the baby's DNA, and that's not without risk, so it will have to wait."

"And you and Merk are twins, so DNA is already muddled. How close is she to giving birth?"

Terk looked at him in surprise, knowing that Merk was not involved in this, not in that way. "I didn't ask," Terk replied, "and it's been weeks. I better find that out." Then he shook his head. "Jesus, that will be one more person in danger over this bullshit," he wailed. "And I'm damn tired of it."

"Yeah, me too." Scott looked back toward Naira's room. "I'll stay. I'll ask for a cot. I'll rest every time she does. Just as she helped me, I'll help her." He saw Terk frowning, not liking that answer. "And I'll disconnect from you. I promise."

"You'll need to. Particularly right now because I'm getting very tired."

"I will," Scott promised. "You go back to the compound, or wherever it is you're staying, and figure out what the hell is going on here. We need answers, and we need them fast."

"I'll go back to her hotel. Hopefully that might lead me to something. I'll set up outside security here as well."

Scott didn't like that answer, but he could also see the sense of it. "You won't have any help if you run into trouble though," he murmured.

"My brother is here," Terk noted. "Merk's running solo, so you'll never really know where he is, until all of a sudden he's there."

"Well, if Merk's here," Scott said, feeling better, "that would be a huge help."

"He's been our liaison with MI6," Terk added.

"Oh, wow, you really will owe your brother for this one, won't you?"

At that, Terk cracked a smile. "You have no idea. We keep dropping bodies on them, and they're getting more and more pissed."

"Yeah, but, if it's not you killing them," Scott noted, "what can they do?"

"I hear you, and you're right, but they still don't appreciate all the added business."

"No, they never do," Scott replied. "They really never do."

CHAPTER 5

NAIRA WOKE WITH a start. As she tried to sit up, hands gently pressed her back down again. She stared up at Scott's face. "You?" she asked, bewildered. "What are you doing here? Why?"

"You're hurt," he said, realizing just how much they did need to talk. "I want you to ease back, until you're comfortable. You've got a punctured lung, and it will heal nicely, but it'll take a bit," he murmured. "So you need to rest."

She slowly took a deep breath and then another. "Well, it feels better than the last time I was awake and trying to breathe."

"The good news is that it will improve on a daily basis."

"But you're injured too," she noted, looking at him carefully. He didn't look sick though. How? "You shouldn't be here. You need to be resting."

"I'm here and can rest while you sleep, so I'm staying," he argued. "So don't waste your strength trying to stop me."

She frowned and didn't say anything. Shifting ever-so-slightly and wincing at the pain, she looked around the room. "Where's Terk?"

"He's gone back to your hotel room." She looked up at Scott, and he just shrugged. "He needed a place to crash. Plus he wondered if somebody would try to access your room, in case they were looking for something."

"So, he set himself up as bait?" she asked, her tone flat.

"Well, it's hardly bait if he goes in prepared. He's not alone either."

"Good. He's special."

Scott nodded. Terk connected with people on a deeper level than most did. If Terk were asked about what that special something was, he'd say, *What are you talking about?* He affected people profoundly, and he didn't even realize it. "Terk *is* special," Scott added. "I'm sure he will be fine."

"I'm sure he will," she murmured. "He's just that kind of guy."

She looked over at him. "I'm sorry."

"For what?" he asked quietly.

"You know what for," she replied. And the moodiness to her tone had him groaning. "We should always communicate," she said.

"Well, that went out the window when you got married."

"When I got married at my father's request, you mean?"

"Your father has always been a bit of a bastard and a manipulator too," Scott murmured.

"Yet you and I both know that I owe him."

"You don't owe him shit," Scott declared, with feeling. "He's your father, so looking after you is what he should be doing, not you looking after him."

"Well, it worked in a sense—to stabilize the company, I mean. Stocks were fine. He didn't lose his shit, *blah, blah, blah,*" she stated.

"And your marriage?"

"Well, it was a mistake right from the beginning," she admitted. "And I learned pretty quickly that my husband had no intention of honoring the vows. So, whatever."

"Ah. … But, for you, it was a real marriage?"

"I was prepared to give it my all. We'd always been friends," she noted. "So marriage didn't seem like it was the worst idea in the world."

"And now?"

"Now it seems like it was the worst idea in the world," she admitted, "and I really don't understand how I came to make that kind of a decision."

"Neither do I."

"I get that," she said, looking over at him. "I get that you don't understand, but it's not as if we were a thing."

"And here I thought we were a thing," he muttered, surprised that she knew what he was thinking.

"Well, if we were," she added, "you weren't doing anything about it."

"Let me ask you something," he murmured, looking at her. "Did you?"

She stared at him, not comprehending for a moment. "Did I what?"

"Did you do anything to further our relationship?"

Naira flushed. "No. … I didn't."

"Neither of us did. We were walking this pathway, lurching along, as if somebody would do something about it, and neither of us did."

"So why are you so angry at me then?" she murmured.

"Because I'd been planning on doing something about it," he replied. "Just like I think, in your mind, you'd been planning on me doing something about it too."

She sighed. "Maybe, but all you had to do was say, *Don't*, and I wouldn't have married him."

He stopped and looked at her. "Seriously?" Scott shook his head. "Because hearing that right now sounds pretty shitty."

"I mean it," she said. "I was rather desperately hoping that you would stop me and would ask me to marry you instead or something. But you didn't say anything, and I thought you looked like you were completely disinterested."

"Well, the woman I loved had just told me that she was marrying somebody else, so what the hell did you expect me to do?" He spoke with just enough bitterness that he realized just how much he was still affected by this one fateful event. He groaned. *Why didn't she just say all this before the wedding?* "This is not a discussion we should be having right now. You need to focus on healing."

She laughed and then cried out at the pain. "God," she said, as she gasped. "Pretty sure I told you that yesterday."

"Pretty sure I told you the day before too," he noted cheerfully.

She stared at him. "I've lost that much time?"

"Yes, but you also gained an awful lot more," he reminded her. "You're alive, so stay focused on what's important." He got up, used the washroom; when he came back, she remained in the same position. "Do you need anything?" he asked her.

"Well, a new life would be good," she stated. "Apparently I blew up the one that I had."

"I don't think you've blown up anything," Scott admitted, "but you made some choices that affect a lot of other people. So, if things weren't exactly smooth, that could be why."

"It feels like they'll never get smooth again," she said.

"Maybe not. No way to know."

"You won't make it easy on me either, will you?"

"Trust is harder," he stated, "particularly after it's been

broken."

"I could say the same," she replied. "I was pretty devastated when I told you, and you didn't have anything to say about it."

"It's not as if you told me that you didn't want to marry him or that you were looking for a way to get out of your father's manipulations," he murmured.

"No, but it never occurred to me that I needed to do that with you."

"And it never occurred to you that you could just stand up to your father and tell him no?" He stared at her. "You came to me. Remember?" Scott said in disbelief. "You were the one sitting in front of me, telling me that you *would* marry somebody else."

"Yes, I get that," she snapped in a harsh voice. "Believe me. I'm still not even sure how I decided that was something I needed to do. But all it would have taken was one word from you."

"And how much did you expect me to argue?" he asked. "Did you really think I would ask you to change your mind, when it was obvious you'd already made up your mind?"

"But I hadn't made up my mind," she argued, "and I think I was really just using that to help push you forward." Her voice held a bitterness he wasn't expecting.

"What do you mean?"

"I think I was trying to make you say it should be us instead, but, when you didn't say anything, I realized that nobody gave a shit, so I might as well marry him after all," she murmured. "So you see? It really did backfire on me."

SCOTT WASN'T SURE he could believe what he was hearing. "We never used to play games like that."

"No, and I'm not even sure whether or not it was my idea." Naira frowned, as she looked off into the distance.

"Probably that bloody father of yours."

"No, he would get someone else to do it. So probably someone else in the family." And then she winced. "I think it was."

"Well, the rest of your family was just as messed up."

She snorted at that.

He shrugged. "You know it as well as I do."

"Unfortunately I think you're quite right."

He nodded. "Every one of them are all about manipulations and lies."

"It's the business," she explained.

"Well, that's *not* how I do business."

"No," she murmured. "It's not how I want to do business either, but, for them, it's all about stocks and exchange, as a business perspective. If we were perceived to be stable and merging our companies," she noted, "then everybody would believe that the stocks would calm down. They had been extremely volatile up until then."

"Sure, but the market has an awful lot of shit going on too. If stocks were volatile, you make adjustments elsewhere to restore confidence."

"That's what we were trying to do," she said. "We were trying to calm them down."

"So, what happened afterward?" he asked.

"They calmed down." She nodded. "So, I mean, in that sense, it worked."

He nodded, not really sure what to say at that point.

"Was it the right thing to do? I don't know," she admitted. "I don't like games like that. At the same time, it's over. I am divorced, and that's hardly an issue anymore."

"And, in that divorce, did the stocks get volatile again?" he asked her.

"No, I think the general public had moved on, and we weren't under the microscope anymore."

"Interesting that you were deemed the only answer in the first place," Scott said.

"Yeah, well, again, it's not my thing, but sometimes the spotlight turns in your direction, and somehow, all of a sudden, people look at you differently. It just takes somebody saying one thing, and it can all go to shit real fast."

He nodded. "You're right, it can, but you still didn't need to marry the guy."

"No, I didn't," she agreed, "but, when you didn't seem to care one bit, well, it didn't make a difference either way. So I went ahead with it, for my father's sake."

"And what about your relationship with your father now?"

She winced. "He passed away."

"Oh." Scott stared at her in fascination. "I'm sorry about that."

"I'm sorry that you didn't see him at the end," she murmured. "You would have appreciated what he had to say."

"I highly doubt that. Your dad never liked me."

"That may be true," she agreed, "but he certainly came to understand one thing at the end of his life."

"And what was that?" Scott asked curiously.

"He understood where my heart was, and he was sorry that he ever got involved."

"A little late for that, wasn't it?" Scott asked her, with

that same tone he'd used before.

She flinched, making him feel like a heel. "He was a lot of things," she admitted, "and difficult was definitely one of them. I really understood just how difficult since he's been gone."

"All because you're unfettered now?" Scott asked. "What about your ex? Still in touch with your old friend?"

"I don't know how he's doing," she replied. "I didn't head up any of the business, so I don't really have very much to do with any of them anymore."

"Not even your mother-in-law or your stepmother?"

"No, definitely not them," she said, "and, of course, my stepsister is a whole different ball game."

"Why? What's she up to?"

She hesitated and then added, "I think she's marrying my ex."

He looked at her, and then he started to laugh and laugh. "Oh my God, that's priceless. That's probably what they should have done in the first place."

She shrugged. "Believe me. That had occurred to me. But I needed out myself, so …" She shrugged and didn't finish the rest of the sentence.

"Well, you're out now," he murmured. "As long as you stay out, you'll be okay."

"That's my intention," she replied, "but it's not always that easy."

"Nothing is easy about this relationship stuff." Scott stared at her hard. "Particularly trying to reclaim some past history."

"I know," she said. "I know you don't want anything to do with me, and I'm sorry because I really messed things up."

"Marrying someone else tends to do that," he muttered.

She nodded. "I get it. I really do, but I appreciate your sitting here to make sure I'm okay. I am better, so you can go off and lead your life in whatever it is that you're doing right now," she said, "though I'm pretty sure it will be all about vengeance at the moment."

"I don't know about vengeance." Scott stared at her, trying to figure out just what he was doing here. "But I'm not leaving until the doctor says that you're cleared, and we have a safe place for you to go. Terk will also arrange security outside your door here, but that's not set up yet."

"That responsibility should be mine, though I came over here because of you."

"Exactly," Scott agreed, "and, if you hadn't been here, you wouldn't have been shot."

"And again, not your problem," she reminded him in a colder tone than he expected. "If anything," she added, "that's on Terk."

CHAPTER 6

NAIRA WOKE UP the next time, only to discover she was alone. Immediately her heart sank, and then the anguish kicked in. He said that he would stay, but she had told him not to, so why should she be so surprised? Still, it hurt to think that he could walk away quite so easily. As soon as Terk had called her to let her know of Scott's accident, she'd come running, but apparently Scott didn't have the same level of attachment.

Even as she thought about that, she knew it didn't fit with the man she had seen at her bedside this whole time. But not seeing him here now was enough to send her off in a tailspin again. Her moods were all over the place, and that wasn't good. She had to find balance in all this craziness and to acknowledge the fact that, somewhere along the line, it seemed like maybe something was between them still, or she had hoped so at least. Maybe she was just looking for forgiveness; she didn't know.

When the door opened, Naira shifted to see a nurse walking in.

The nurse's face lit up. "You're awake," she said, with a smile. "That's very good to see."

"Have I been out long?"

The nurse shrugged. "Off and on, yes," she replied, "but this is the first time you're looking like you're really here."

"I can't imagine how I must have looked before," Naira noted.

The nurse laughed. "Hey, it's what we expect. You were still dealing with a lot of drugs from the surgery, not to mention the pain meds."

"Which I didn't even realize I had."

"We had to get the bullet out," she explained. "How are you feeling?"

"Still in a lot of pain," she murmured.

"That's to be expected, and we can manage that. No need for you to be uncomfortable."

Naira wondered at that term because how did she *not* feel uncomfortable when she just had surgery after being shot?

"Oh, and in case you're wondering," the nurse added, "your lover boy is sitting outside in the hallway on the phone."

She looked at her in surprise. "Scott's here?"

"Yeah, he hasn't left your side this whole time," the nurse confirmed, "and we do love to see that."

"Why?" she asked curiously.

"Simple, because it's good for you. To know you are loved helps keep your focus on healing," she murmured. She busied herself checking all of Naira's stats. "You know what? Your vitals are really quite good," she shared, "considering what you've been through. The doctor is scheduled to be here soon, probably in about an hour or so."

Mentally Naira added another hour to that, since, in her experience, doctors were rarely on time or consistent. But she nodded, thanked the nurse, and asked, "Any chance for a cup of coffee?"

"That's another good sign," the cheerful nurse noted,

with a bright smile. "An appetite and a return to normal types of events."

"Is coffee considered a normal type of event?" she asked with half a smile.

"Well, if it's the first thing you wake up for in the morning," she replied, "I would think so." And, with that, she disappeared.

As the nurse walked out, Scott walked in. He looked at her, smiled, and said, "Now you're looking better."

"Is that what a little sleep does?" she asked and then stifled a yawn.

"Yep, it sure does," he agreed, studying her.

"Any news?" she murmured.

"Some, MI6 is interviewing the rest of the team right now."

"Great." Then seeing his expression, she asked, "Or is that not a great idea?" As she studied his face, she realized he was looking pretty worn out himself. "There's absolutely no point in your being here," she said crossly, "particularly if it'll hurt you more."

He shook his head. "I'm fine."

She snorted. "Good try," she replied, "but *fine* is not a word I would use to describe your own features this morning."

"I'm a little tired, no doubt," he agreed cheerfully, "but that was due to some shifts in energy I had to make." She gave him a flat stare, and he shrugged. "I'm sure you heard some of the conversations I had with Terk yesterday—or the day before."

"Honestly I'm not even sure when any of that was," she admitted. "It's all a big jumble."

"In that case, just leave it be," he said, with a bright

smile.

"In other words, you won't tell me more."

"The less you know about some things, the better," he murmured.

She shook her head. "That's just you trying to keep me out of it." At that, she saw him closing off slightly. She nodded. "And that's exactly what you're thinking. I knew it. Fine." She stared around the room. "How soon can I go home?"

"Not very soon at all," he stated calmly. "Not until we sort out this whole thing."

"Well, that's not for you to decide. So, as soon as the doctor releases me," she stated, "I'm going home." In reality, the hurt she felt was so acute that she wanted him to leave so she could bawl some more. She knew in her heart of hearts that this would be the end of any possibility of *us*, and she needed that good old British stiff upper lip to get through it. Too bad her British stiff upper lip syndrome had become very Americanized over the last many years.

"While you're here," Scott began, "are you planning on seeing any family?"

"No," she declared in a harsh tone. "I don't have any plans to see them at all."

He nodded slowly. "That's too bad. I could let you go, if you had a place to stay close by."

"Doesn't matter since it's not up to you to let me go," she argued, with more intensity than she'd expected. But then, seeing the look on his face and having him shutting her out, what did he expect?

"Terk can talk to you about it later," Scott added.

"He might be your friend and your boss, but he's not mine," she snapped.

Just then the door opened, and another woman walked in. Looking at Naira, she said, "Hello. Remember me? Let's have a look."

"As soon as he's gone," Naira stated.

The doctor looked at Scott, and obediently he got up and walked out.

"You really don't want him here?" the doc asked. "I'm surprised at that, since he's been such a mainstay during your visit with us."

The fact that the doc had used the term *visit* made Naira want to laugh. "Visit? Is that what this is?" she teased.

"Okay, well, either way, you ended up here in the hospital, and he's been sitting at your side, worrying ever since."

"Yet he just made it very clear that it's not personal, and he's feeling guilty," she shared dismissively. "We had some problems between us, and I was hoping it would get resolved, but it doesn't look like it. So all I really want to do is leave."

The doctor pursed her lips, as she considered Naira for a long moment. "The thing is," she explained, "we want you to stay for another few days, and I don't want to release you if you don't have somewhere local to go."

"That's my problem," she declared. "I'll be fine." When the doctor hesitated, Naira looked at her and asked, "Do you have any reason to keep me?" And she knew that she was being overly harsh in tone, which wasn't very polite to this woman who had quite possibly saved Naira's life. "Otherwise I would just as soon go back to my hotel and rest and recover there."

"Even at that," the doc replied, "if you ran into trouble, nobody is there to help you."

"I can come back in a few days to be checked, if that

would make you feel any better."

"You'd have to come to my office," she stated.

"Fine, I can get there, I'm sure. I'll get a cab or something."

"Well, let's see how you're doing tomorrow." And, with that, the doc was gone.

Frowning, not liking the fact that everybody seemed to want Naira to stay close, when she didn't want to be here, just added to her frustration. When Scott walked back in again, she told him, "The doctor is releasing me tomorrow, and I'm going back to my hotel. I promised to stay in town for a few days for her to keep an eye on me."

He looked at her and then nodded. "That's fine. I'm sure we can set up some kind of security at a hotel for you."

"I hardly think that's necessary," she suggested, trying to be friendly, but her stiff manner was something she wasn't prepared to ease up on. They had no right to keep her here, and she would make sure they had no way to do so.

He gazed at her steadily. "You know we're only doing this for your own good, right?"

"Wow," she said in a mocking tone. "If I had a penny for every time somebody used that phrase on me … And, yeah, my father's favorite comment was very similar. 'This is for your own good,'" she repeated, rolling her eyes.

"Hey, I'm not your father."

"No, you're not," she replied, "but you are just as manipulative."

He glared at her. "I think it's time I went and got a cup of coffee."

"You do that," she muttered, as he turned to walk out. After that, she settled back and waited for her coffee. She just wanted this to be over, so she could get back to some semblance of normality, whatever that would mean in her new world. It just seemed like everything was going wrong right now.

When Scott returned, he looked at her and frowned. "I don't want us to fight."

"Good." She waved her hand at him. "Let me go then."

"You know what?" he said, with just a tinge of sadness to his tone. "I don't think I can."

She opened her eyes and stared at him in shock. "What are you talking about?"

"It's not as if we don't have a lot of history to go through."

"We have no history," she argued, "at least none that's worth bringing up anymore."

He stared at her. "I guess if we wanted to start again," he suggested, "we would *both* need to move on from the past."

"Since you're not prepared to do that," she stated, "it's really not an issue to bring up."

"And yet," he murmured, "you're not there either."

"In what way?"

He shrugged. "I think you still blame yourself."

She stared at him, her eyebrows shooting up. "Did I say I blamed myself for something?"

"Yes," he declared. "Maybe for not making it clear what it was you were looking for from me. Maybe for allowing your father to manipulate you into a sham marriage. Maybe for allowing yourself to decide to make the best of it. But, of course, making the best of something is not the same thing as having what you want."

She stared at him, feeling something inside her trying hard to shut down the conversation, but, at the same time, she was fascinated because it was the first time Scott had broached anything about their history so directly. "Why are you even bringing this up?" she asked quietly. "You don't want anything to do with me, and you've made that very clear."

He snorted. "Well, just like you," he replied, "sometimes we have to consider where we're at and what we're doing."

"No," she disagreed, "we really don't."

He frowned. "Are you happy to just leave?"

"That's what I'm trying to do," she said, with a note of humor, "but nobody seems to want to let me go."

"No," he agreed, "and for good reason. I don't think this is a good way to end things between us."

"Well, it's probably better than the last time," she muttered.

He winced at that. "You're right there," he confirmed, "but that was not an easy time for either of us. I was pretty angry."

She snorted. "I was pretty devastated too. It was obvious that you didn't give a shit and that I'd been pinning my hopes on a relationship that you didn't give a crap about."

"Hardly," he murmured. Just then his phone buzzed with a text message, and he looked down and froze.

"What's the matter?" she asked.

He sighed. "There's been another attack on one of the team members," he replied, "when they were heading out for supplies."

"Supplies?" she asked, with an eyebrow up. "What kind of supplies did they have to get?"

He rolled his eyes. "A lot of them are living and working together," he murmured. "So, in theory, they need a lot of groceries to keep everybody fed, for one thing."

"Is that why Terk came in and then left again?"

"Most likely. He didn't tell me."

"Well, it is what it is," she muttered.

When the nurse walked in, she was carrying coffee. Naira looked at her, smiled, and said, "Thank you. You have no idea how much I appreciate this." The nurse smiled in return, gave it to her, and left.

Naira sat here, sipping it, barely realizing when Scott got up and left. As soon as the door closed, she felt herself relaxing. It was hard to even be close to him, and she realized what kind of problems they had between them and the stress of not being able to resolve them. There was really no righting this. Was he correct? Was she feeling guilty? Probably, she had made life decisions that had a terminal effect on their relationship. Of course that's not what she had wanted, but she'd also been younger in so many ways. And who knows? Maybe she needed to go through something like this. Maybe she needed to be such an idiot in order to realize that so much more was involved in life. Regardless it was just frustrating.

When Scott walked back in again, she saw from the look on his face that he needed to leave. She shooed him away. "Go on. I'm safe here," she stated. "Go deal with whatever you've got to deal with." He hesitated, as she shook her head. "There's really no point in staying."

He snorted at that. "You've already been attacked once," he noted. "And we have no way to know if another attack's coming. We have a shift change in your security guard, so I'm staying."

"They have no reason to attack me again," she replied. "Your friends, however, appear to be a bigger issue, so go and deal with it."

He just glared at her.

She shrugged. "I'm just staying here and drinking coffee. The doctor won't even let me out of here until tomorrow." She saw that Scott was torn, but she didn't know quite how to push him to get him to go. Finally she finished her coffee, put it on the table at her side, then slipped down lower in the bed, shuddering at the pain. "I'll sleep, so do whatever you want. You always do."

With that, she closed her eyes resolutely and let herself drift off into dreamland.

SCOTT ALMOST GROWLED. Naira was so damn frustrating when she got into a mood like this. The fact that Scott had shared as much as he had also showed him that he was dealing with some issues too. But she was right. He did want to go. He wanted to get back to his team, but he also wanted to take her with him. But he wasn't sure that the team would be ready for that. Another stranger was a lot to absorb, especially when everybody was already on edge.

Terk had been here but had abruptly disappeared, and now Scott had no idea where his boss had gone. Scott had sent out a message, asking for information, but, so far, nobody had come back with an answer.

Being cut out like this was deadly. Scott kind of understood how she felt because, right now, he was in the same boat. Nobody was bringing him on board because he wasn't up to snuff either. And that was damn frustrating.

Almost frustrating enough for him to take her advice and go, but he also knew that, if anything were to happen to her, there would be hell to pay all around. He was still getting his mind wrapped around the whole forced marriage mess that they'd been through before that led to their breakup. Back then Scott had just come off a job that had been very difficult, and he wasn't even working with Terk's group at that point in time. It had been a case where several men had been killed on a job, and Scott had been recovering, or perhaps not recovering, maybe just being totally morose about the whole thing and about his life in general. He'd been wondering what he was going to do next when she had dropped the marriage bomb on him.

And sure, it had been years ago, and they were both different people now. But were they different enough? He didn't know. He only knew that whenever he made any attempt to leave her, he found himself still sitting here, doing nothing about her. And that didn't bode well for his future. Especially since she didn't appear to want to talk about anything that was important to them. But then, why would she?

Scott wished he hadn't been so nonreceptive the first couple times they had spoken, before she had been so hurt from his lack of response. And that said something about him that he needed to consider. Did it really take somebody getting shot for him to realize what was important in his life? Or to see an olive branch when it was being offered? But still, he hadn't offered one back, and that was the problem. And now that he was attempting to, she wasn't exactly listening.

He groaned as he sat here, wishing that something would break. Something that would stop him from sitting here like an idiot, waiting for her to wake up again. Knowing that, even when she did wake up, nothing would be changed between them. It was a sad fact, but they were all in the middle of whatever nightmare was going on, and it wasn't clear what the end of this would look like.

When his phone rang, he jumped on it. "Hey," he whispered to Terk, as Scott stepped out into the hallway. "Everybody okay?"

"Yes," he replied, "but MI6 is pissed. One of their guys caught a random bullet."

"Is he dead?"

"No, he's not. But, if these guys had wanted to keep anything quiet, they just blew that chance."

"I'm surprised you even got MI6 in on the deal."

"Not really sure we had much choice at this point, being on their turf," Terk explained. "Plus we kept finding so many bodies that Merk couldn't keep Jonas off the case anymore."

"I get it," Scott said.

After a moment of silence, Terk asked, "How is she?"

"Hurting, back asleep at the moment. *Fine* is what she'd say," he huffed, with half a shrug. "It's hard to say how she really is though."

"Have you had a chance to talk to her?"

"Yes, but she's not terribly receptive."

Terk laughed. "So when she wakes up again, approach her again," he suggested. "You guys need to sort this out."

"She's asked to leave the hospital and to go to a hotel for a few days," he told Terk, "and then she wants to go home."

"Of course she does," Terk agreed. "Where is home now anyway?"

"I didn't even ask," Scott admitted, feeling like an idiot. "For all I know, home is England. That's where her family was anyway."

"So, that would make sense in some ways," Terk said.

"Maybe. Except she doesn't want anything to do with

them. Nothing about this makes a whole lot of sense, if you ask me," Scott replied.

"Maybe not, but stay the course for now," Terk suggested. "There's a good chance this could all work out in your favor."

"It sure doesn't feel like it," Scott muttered. "It feels like I blew it."

"If you did, only you can fix it," Terk stated in that same calm and logical voice that he had for everything.

Scott glared at the phone. "It's not that easy."

"It's never that easy," Terk noted. "But it's up to you to make your feelings clear. Then at least she'd have a chance to make a fully informed decision, one way or another."

"What happened to *my* chance to make a fully informed decision?" he protested.

"You already made it," Terk said. "Look where you are." And, with that, he hung up.

Scott paced the hallway. It didn't take him long to realize that Terk was right. Scott didn't know what that said about him, except for the fact that it really did mean that, as far as he was concerned, if he had another chance with Naira, he would take it. But how could he convince her of that?

Listening to her explanation had been an eye opener, and it eased some of the long-held blame and resentment that he'd found himself holding close. It was much easier to hug blame than it was to look at his own behavior. He hadn't been in great emotional shape back then. Hell, he hadn't been in great emotional shape for a long time after that point.

Once he'd started working for Terk, Scott learned to open up his different skills to see how he could make a difference in his life. And he realized that even just opening up that much had made a huge impact on his mental abilities. He was sure the shrinks would have a lot to say about that; Scott just didn't want to listen to it. Hell, he hadn't wanted to listen to shrinks in a very long time. He wasn't about to start now, though maybe he should. He cringed at the thought.

"Hell no," he grumbled, as he pushed that thought out of his mind again. As he paced, he wandered down to the emergency room and cafeteria area, where he picked himself up another cup of coffee. As he came back out, an ambulance pulled in, with MI6 close behind. Apparently this was the agent who had been shot. Scott winced as he watched. He recognized a couple of the officers, but he stayed in the shadows. No point in getting them all riled up if they saw him, but it was too late.

One of them took one look at him and raced toward him. "Hey," Sam said, with a big smile. "I had no idea you are alive and well."

"Well, alive, yes. But *well?* I'm not so sure about," he said.

"What are you doing here? Are you still in the hospital?"

"No, a friend of mine got shot yesterday—or maybe even the day before," Scott said, shaking his head. "It seems like I'm losing my mind."

"Jesus, you're mixed up in that whole mess where Stoop here got shot, aren't you?"

"If you mean the work you've been doing with Merk and his brother, Terk, then yes," Scott said. "That's one word for it."

"What a nightmare that is."

Scott nodded. "Did you guys catch the shooter?"

"No, but you can bet we're after him now, once he starts

going after our officers," Sam declared, shaking his head.

"It's a real shitstorm out there. Sorry you're caught up in it."

"Yeah, same here." Sam hesitated, looking at the emergency room doors. "I want to stay and talk but …"

"Give me your number," Scott said, "and I'll let you know when he's out. I can keep watch for you." Sam hesitated, then he shrugged. "Look," Scott began. "We're all on the same side, and apparently you guys were brought in because of what's going on in my world. So I can easily do you this much of a favor."

Sam still hesitated, then he nodded. "Here's my card. But I mean it, you let me know the minute there's a change."

"Will do. Let's hope that he'll be just fine and will wake up pissing mad that he's even in here."

"That's exactly how he would be too," the MI6 agent noted, with a smile. And, with that, he was gone.

Now with two people to keep an eye on, Scott walked back and forth between the two floors on a regular basis, checking in on both of them. When the agent was sent in for surgery, he quickly sent a message off to Sam, letting him know that Stoop was heading into surgery. He got a thumbs-up in reply but nothing else. But, hey, Scott was doing what he could. It just sucked that even what he was doing wasn't very much.

When he wandered back upstairs to her floor, he saw a man loitering at the end of the hallway. Then the nurse raced toward the guy, laughing and smiling. He put his arms around her, gave her a quick peck on the cheek, and then the two of them disappeared down the stairs. Scott was suspicious of everything. His instinctive thought had been that maybe the guy was back for a second attempt at killing

Naira. It just made no sense to even bother trying at a hospital.

He sent Terk a question, asking about Nurse Nancy, who had been taking care of Scott.

Terk sent a text back, letting him know that she was fine and had left town.

Scott figured that was probably better than to have her still here and a target too, what with everything else going on. Because nothing here looked like it was good news at all. With that, he headed toward Naira's room. Her door was partially open, and Naira lay unconscious, collapsed on the floor.

CHAPTER 7

N AIRA WOKE TO the sound of somebody crying. She struggled to the surface and realized the crying was coming from her own throat. She surfaced, with a gasp, finding she was in Scott's arms, held close, somebody else right beside him. "What happened?" she asked in a shaky voice.

"I left you alone," he said, his tone grim.

She tried to comprehend what he was saying, but it just didn't make any sense. She closed her eyes, as somebody added the contents of a syringe into her IV line. She heard voices around, but Scott was whispering to her.

"Just go to sleep," he said.

Gratefully she went under.

When she surfaced again, she noted her head was swaddled, and needles were in her arm. She groaned and fell asleep. Once again she tried to surface, and immediately there was Scott. She looked at him. "Did I get hurt again?" she asked. "Or did I have some sort of a reaction?"

"You were hurt again," he replied, his tone still grim. "I was downstairs at the emergency room, came up here again, and was distracted by somebody in the hallway. When I came into your room, you had either fallen or had been attacked."

"Which was it?" she demanded. "And don't lie to me."

He gave her a half smile. "I had no intention of lying," he said, "but the jury is out as to what happened, until they checked your blood and found you had been injected with something," he murmured.

"What kind of something?"

"They've sent it for a tox screen, and we don't yet know, but they did a full flush of your system, as they tried to get you back again," he replied.

She stared up at him, as hot tears of despair ran down her cheeks. "What did I ever do to them?" she whispered.

"I'm not sure," Scott admitted. "I'm trying to get to the bottom of why they are still after you."

She nodded slowly. "Unless I saw something, or they think I saw something," she murmured, as she lay against his chest.

"Did you?" he asked her suddenly.

"Did I what?" she murmured, closing her eyes.

"Did you see something?"

Her eyes opened slowly. "How would I know?" she asked, shuddering, as she twisted to look up at him. "How am I supposed to know if I saw something important or not?"

"Maybe you should take me back through what you did see," he suggested.

"I don't even know where to begin," she murmured. "I took a taxi from the airport to the hotel, and Terk picked me up from there."

"And when you saw Terk, was anybody around him, anybody nearby?"

She frowned and muttered. "It looked like he was alone," she replied, "but how am I supposed to know that?"

"Did you see any unusual activity or see anyone in particular?"

She tried to shake her head and then winced. "No, I don't think so, nothing unusual anyway." She waited a moment. "I was pretty distracted and had come all this way because you were hurt," she murmured. "I was pretty shook up over the whole thing."

"I can understand that," he agreed. "And I'm sorry."

"It's not your fault," she murmured.

"It is now that you're here, injured."

"Well, maybe," she agreed, "if that makes you feel better. Honestly I just want to feel better myself."

He shifted so she was back down on her hospital bed.

She yawned. "Did the attacker give me something to knock me out?"

"They hit you over the head and stabbed you with a needle, so I'm not too sure what their plan was."

"Well, it's not as if they'll take me away from here," she noted. "You don't just carry somebody out of a hospital, and they would seem to have no purpose for keeping me alive."

"I don't know what's going on here," Scott murmured, "but I won't leave you alone again."

She nodded. "I don't even remember what happened last time. I remember the nurse came in. She was young, smiling, happy," Naira shared. "I felt kind of blue and down, but she was definitely perky."

"Was it the same nurse you'd seen before?"

"No," Naira replied, "it wasn't. I didn't recognize her at all."

"*Hmm.*" Scott frowned.

"What? Do you think she did something? I don't re-member when she left though," Naira added, frowning as more memories filtered through. "She was giving me a shot."

Scott looked at her in surprise. "Did she say what it was?"

At that, Naira shook her head. "No, I don't know that she said anything at all."

"Interesting," Scott replied. "Maybe I'll talk to the doctor and see what was scheduled."

She stopped and looked at him. "Do you think it was her?"

"I'm not sure," he admitted, "but somebody was in here, and, when I came up the stairs, I was distracted by a young couple at the end of the hallway. A guy was waiting, and she raced toward him, gave him a big kiss, and then they left."

"Interesting," she murmured. "Do you think that was a cover?"

"At this point in time," he muttered, "it is quite possible. I don't want to take any chances."

"Well, I'd appreciate it if you didn't," she replied, "but we also can't assume anything at this point."

"No, I get that," he murmured. "I just don't want you hurt again."

She certainly agreed with that. But his ability to keep her safe appeared to be severely compromised. If these other guys were serious, they would find her. "I don't even know what the reason could be for attacking me," she murmured. "It's not as if I know anything."

"And you don't think that you've seen anything that would be suspicious?"

"No," she replied.

He nodded thoughtfully.

"What are you thinking?" she asked, looking at him.

"I'm just wondering if they think that you're involved in some way," he murmured.

"Nothing is making sense," she murmured, as she stretched out on the bed. "But now I have a terrible headache, and I really don't like the idea of staying here in the hospital anymore."

"No, that's no longer an option," he agreed.

She rolled her head over, so she could look at him more closely. "What will we do about it then?" she asked.

"It's already in process," he replied. "I'm just waiting for clearance."

She frowned, but then his phone buzzed. As she listened, it sounded like whatever arrangements were being made had been successfully completed. Scott stood, walked to the closet, and pulled out her clothes. She stared at his movements. "Now that's one fine bloody mess of clothes."

"It is," Scott agreed, "and, for that, I'm sorry. We'll get you new clothes when we get out of here."

She slowly pulled back the covers and sat up, but her head really boomed. "And now, for the first time, as much as I wanted to leave the hospital, it won't be an easy transition."

"No, it won't," Scott stated, "and, if I thought staying here would be safer, I'd wait."

"But you think they'll come back?"

"Yes," he stated, "I do."

Using the bed rail for support, she slowly stood, and the room swayed around her. "Dear God," she whispered. "This isn't quite how I expected to be leaving."

"And it's not how you should be leaving," he murmured, "but we don't really have any good options right now."

"I can't imagine the hospital is very happy either."

"No, they aren't. You were attacked under their roof, so they're not very happy at all."

She nodded at that. Then, with Scott's help, she made

her way to the bathroom, where he left her alone to slowly get changed into her bloody clothes.

As she stepped out, he looked at her critically. "You're on your feet, and you're moving, so I'll take that as a good sign."

She wasn't sure she would, but, if he was happy, well, okay. Still, she had hoped to leave and to go to a hotel for a couple days to recuperate and to be a hell of a lot better off. Now it was as if she'd taken a firm step backward. She made several steps toward the door, when he grabbed her gently and said, "Nope."

She frowned at him and asked, "No *what?*"

He pointed to the wheelchair, and she looked at it in disgust. He shook his head. "This is not the time for ego, okay?"

She countered, "If that was you, no way in hell you'd be going out in a wheelchair."

"It's a long walk," he added. "No way you'll make that trip on your own."

She wouldn't even argue further and just slumped into the chair, collapsing back. "You're right," she murmured, "and I feel just crappy enough that I really don't care anymore."

He nodded, placed her purse in her lap, and replied, "That's the spirit. Let's just get you out safe."

She snorted. "And I thought being here was safe."

"We did too, but we weren't expecting anybody to come back after you, and that means a whole different story."

She nodded. "I get it. So when do I get to meet all the rest of this team?"

"I don't know," Scott admitted. "Maybe now."

She looked at him, as he wheeled her out the door and

into a really big elevator. "Are we in the service elevator?" she asked in confusion.

"We are and for a good reason."

"Says you," she muttered. But quickly she was whisked into an SUV at the car park level, with Scott and her sharing the back seat. Suddenly they were out onto the street and free. She took several deep breaths. "Now I'm not sure whether this is freedom or not," she noted, half joking. "I didn't expect it to come with a headache."

"Lately it always comes with a headache," replied Terk, who had waited in the driver's seat for them.

"I get that," she murmured. "I really do. I just thought that maybe all of that stage would be over."

"We all did." Terk studied her for a moment. "How are you feeling?"

"Like somebody hit me over the head," she muttered.

He nodded. "We'll have answers about that pretty soon."

"Says you," she murmured. "If you had answers, you'd have given them to me already."

He chuckled. "You sound an awful lot like Scott."

"Like hell," she muttered. "He is stubbornly irritating."

At that, Terk could barely stifle his own laughter.

She glared at him. "I hope you don't think this is funny."

"Nope, not at all," he confirmed. "Attacks on anybody around us are never funny. But the idea that you're not as stubborn and not as irritating as Scott, well, you know what? I'm not really one to insult a lady," he stated. "However, the two of you look like you were made for each other."

She settled back, then looked over at Scott to see him staring out the window, ignoring her. "You may be right," she admitted, "at least on the stubborn part." She tried to follow their route but very quickly lost her way in the ups and downs and ins and outs, as they traveled quickly and then changed direction. "Are you really expecting us to be followed?" she asked Terk in astonishment.

"Let's just say, we aren't taking any chances."

She agreed with that careful philosophy, but, at the same time, it did make her feel a little odd, as they went through back alleys. Suddenly Terk pulled into what looked like a huge complex of warehouses. "What is this?" she asked, for the first time feeling a hint of unease.

"It's our new compound, at least for now," Terk replied.

Scott looked around. "It's the first I've been here too."

She nodded. "And we're safe here?"

"Safer here than anywhere," Terk stated, "and we have lots of people to help defend us here."

"Well, that's good," she muttered. "Because, so far, I don't feel that I'm doing very well in that department."

She missed the look on Scott's face, but when Terk quietly said, "It wasn't his fault," Naira turned to Scott, realizing what she'd implied. "Scott, I didn't mean that how it sounded," she explained. "I didn't mean that you're responsible for this."

"But I am though," he replied, "so let's just not get into that discussion."

"Fine," she muttered, wondering how long it would be before they could tolerate even being in the same room together. She wasn't sure what was going on, but, at the same time, she was out of patience and was too damn exhausted to give a crap. Scott helped her out of the SUV and led the way, pausing behind Terk as they moved toward the inner part of the compound.

She looked around and asked, "People live here? It's like an industrial complex of warehouses."

"It is," Terk confirmed, "and that, in a sense, is a good thing."

She didn't even know what to say. They entered this warehouse—a huge open space, completely empty. They continued to walk through to another area, finding a relaxed living area and a huge kitchen. When they stepped inside, what had been a buzz of noise immediately stopped, and then a woman cried out, raced over, and threw her arms around Scott. What was even more upsetting to Naira was that Scott's arms immediately closed around the woman just as quickly.

The others gathered around, patting Scott on the back, murmuring greetings.

Naira watched carefully as Scott held the woman in his arms and whispered, "It's good to see you, Tasha."

She leaned back and looked up at him, beaming. "Gosh, I was so afraid we'd lost you."

Scott grinned. "I'm a little harder to kill than that," he protested.

"I don't know," she said. "Seems like things have been pretty tough around here lately."

"I'm sorry," he replied. "You've been through a lot. I have too, in a way, but I wasn't even conscious for a lot of it."

She nodded. "If I thought keeping you all unconscious would have kept you healthy, I'd have been all for it."

He rolled his eyes at that. "Yeah, we've just got to get to the bottom of all this." Scott sighed. "Seems like I'm late to the party, but yet I have weird recollections of memories that are post-coma. Regardless I'm here now, and I'll be fine."

With an arm swung toward Naira, he introduced her to everyone.

At that, Tasha turned and looked at the newcomer, then walked over, opened her arms, and gave Naira a gentle hug. "You, my dear, have really been through the wringer." She smiled at her gently.

"Well, I'm really hoping that I'm out drying in the sun now," she murmured.

It took Tasha a few moments to understand the joke, and then she chuckled. "Ha. Oh, I like you already. Come on. Let's get you settled in a room." With that, she led her down the hall to a series of closed doors, with Scott following behind. "We'll put you in here."

Naira stepped in, noting a bathroom was attached to this bedroom. "This is nice." It was sparsely furnished with a chair and a bed, and that's all she really cared about right now. She immediately walked toward the bed and asked, "Would it be rude if I just collapsed for a while?"

"Rude?" Tasha repeated. "No, not at all. You have more people to protect you here, a lot of people and a lot of things going on. If you need to collapse, you collapse. I have a change of clothes waiting for you in the bathroom. I can help you change, if you like?" With a nod from Naira, both women stepped into the bathroom, reappearing shortly thereafter. Tasha helped Naira to the bed. "And I'll tell the others that you'll be out when you're feeling better."

Naira smiled, then lay down on the bed. She felt a chill coming on, but immediately Tasha walked over, picked up an extra blanket that had been on the back of the chair, and spread it over Naira. "Here you go. Having just been injured, you'll be colder than you expect, so make sure you look after yourself. I'll send Scott back in a little bit." And, without giving either of them a chance to argue, Tasha left, taking Scott with her.

Naira closed her eyes and fell asleep.

STANDING AT THE open doorway, Scott watched as Naira collapsed. He closed the door gently behind Tasha. "Thanks for that," he said softly.

She smiled at him. "No problem," she murmured. "You'll find a lot of things have changed too."

"Yeah." He nodded, looking around. "Terk gave me the rundown on some of that. I certainly wasn't expecting such a huge place."

"We need it," she stated. "Our group is expanding."

"I heard, and I'm kind of stunned."

"Well, you can be stunned," Tasha agreed, "but the fact of the matter is that almost everybody has a partner—or at least most of us do. And, depending on how it goes with Naira here, it looks like you do too."

"That's all conjecture at the moment," Scott stated, "and I don't mind saying that I'm not exactly sure myself."

Tasha nodded. "You know what? The path is never straightforward, but, as long as you get there eventually, the journey itself is worthwhile." It sounded cryptic, and she acknowledged it as she looked up and grinned. "Yep, I know. As I said, things have changed."

"It sounds like it," he murmured. "I'm not exactly sure what to think of that. That's not usual talk for you."

"Nothing could be considered 'usual' anymore," she noted, "and that's one of the biggest lessons learned in all this. It's a whole new world. We have several injured members who are still recovering and some who just need rest and relaxation. And," she added, "Terk's trying to hold it all together. Meanwhile he's got a mess going on in Texas that he's still trying to figure out."

"Tell me about Celia," he said. "Jesus, who would even do that to a woman?"

"Not to mention a pregnant one," she reminded him.

Scott winced at that. "And to think she's carrying Terk's child somehow, though of course he doesn't know for sure, does he?"

"It's his," she confirmed, with a weird smile. "You know perfectly well that, if Terk's certain, he's certain."

"I know, but, in something like that, you would think you'd want a little bit more than his version of certainty."

"He would never put the baby at risk, so any traditional testing will just have to wait," Tasha stated. "Anyway, the bottom line is that no one is really 100 percent, and it's not been all that easy for any of us."

"Got it. So, you and Damon, huh?"

She beamed. "*Finally*. It took long enough."

Scott grinned. "Sure, but we all knew it was headed that way."

"Maybe so, but Damon was being stubborn about it."

"Of course he was," Scott agreed. "He was trying to protect you."

"You know what? We do get a little tired of this *trying to protect us* business," she shared. "I get it. I really do, but, at the same time, it's kind of annoying."

Scott walked over when he saw a coffeepot and poured himself a cup, then turned and looked around. "This isn't a bad place to be."

"It's temporary," she murmured. "Alfred helped us get

it. As well as Levi and Ice."

He looked at her with interest. "Alfred's involved?"

"Only on the periphery. So is MI6."

He winced at that reminder and sent a text to Sam. **I'm no longer at hospital. Your friend Stoop was fine when I left.** He immediately got a thumbs-up in return. "Somebody I know from MI6 was at the hospital, asking me to keep an eye on his buddy, who got shot recently. I'm not even sure when all that happened."

"Terk was going to meet the group, but, before he ever got there, they were shot."

"And are they thinking it's part of their meeting with Terk?"

"He's not sure how it could be anything but that," she murmured. "I mean, when you think about it, all of this appears to be connected."

"Which is why I also don't know why they went after Naira twice," he said. "What was the purpose of that?"

"The only thing we can think of is the connection to you." Then she looked back toward the others. "There was a thought that maybe she has abilities."

He looked at Tasha in shock.

"We do have a couple other women here, particularly Cara," Tasha noted, "who kept Rick alive, while he was not doing very well. She's also been contacted by Brody, and she's reverted to using breadcrumbs to try and find him again."

Scott blinked several times, trying to take that in.

Tasha laughed. "Sorry, it's a lot of information. So, if you don't get it the first time around, I understand."

He shook his head. "So they think that maybe Naira's similar to Cara?"

"Yes, and no. There are lots of different abilities, as you well know. But Cara arrived with Terk, and he set up the plans for her to look after Rick."

"Wow," Scott said, startled. "So these guys after the team are taking out anybody connected to us—just in case?"

"It seems like they're trying to take out anybody who's related, leaving no help for us," she agreed. "Almost as if they're petrified that somebody else would have these abilities and could be keeping us alive, as everybody here is supposed to be dead and gone."

Scott took his coffee, walked over to the far side, and sat down. He looked at all the others on the other side of the room, where little groups of people formed at various spots, talking. Scott looked around. "You know that, if anybody were looking for a way to take us all out, this building would be it."

"And we know that," Terk noted, as he separated himself from one of the groups and walked toward them.

Scott looked up at his friend and smiled. "Hey, I forgot to ask. Did you find anything at the hotel?"

"I never made it there," Terk replied. "After she was attacked at the hospital, it just seemed like the best idea was to bring her here."

"I agree with that, but I'm not so sure that she's on board," Scott admitted. "She really wanted to go home."

"That choice was taken away from her with that bullet to the lung," Terk stated, "and we understand that she might not be very happy about it, but, at the same time, she's alive, and that is due to you."

"And yet it seems like all I've done," Scott said, "is hurt her."

"And now you get a chance to help her," Tasha added at

his side.

He looked down and frowned because, of course, they didn't know. She squeezed his arm gently, as if she had a better understanding of what he was going through, and he wasn't exactly sure how any of that worked. But she'd always been a very intuitive, caring person, even more so now.

Just then Damon walked in, caught sight of Scott, then walked over and gave him a big hug. As soon as he stepped back, he looked around, and Tasha was right there. He gave her a hug and kept her tucked up against him. "Good God," Damon said to Scott, "all of us are a mess."

"Yep," Scott agreed, with a nod. "Even when we think it won't be, it's a disaster."

"But why? That is the question I have," Damon noted, crossing his arms. "What in the hell is going on here?"

By the time they finished explaining everything to Scott, he sat here, completely shell-shocked. "You're seriously thinking our government might have hired a contractor to take us all out, and you're thinking that contractor might have been the group we hit in Iran? So somebody survived the Iran attack? Am I following so far?"

At that, Terk nodded.

Scott shot him a look. "What's the point behind all this? Why would our own government want us dead? I just don't get it."

"If I knew the answer to that," Terk replied, "I might sleep at night."

That was the first mention he'd made about not getting sleep, and Scott realized, from the look on everybody else's faces, that they recognized that as a problem as well.

"You need sleep," Damon noted harshly.

"Yeah, well, hopefully one day I'll get it," Terk murmured, "but that day isn't today."

"And why not?" Scott asked. "There's only so much you can do right now."

"A lot of threads need support, and Brody is still lost."

At that, everybody gasped.

"Cara said she found him," Terk added. "Well, she left him breadcrumbs, which he may have found," Terk corrected. "However, he's not surfaced again."

"And what about you? Can you contact him?" Scott asked Terk.

"He's still alive. I can tell you that much," he shared, "but I'm not getting any other response."

"So … it was a one-time event, and Cara blew it?" Wade asked.

At that, Tasha looked over at Wade, a hard expression on her face. "Come on. It's not Cara's fault. You don't get to blame her." He had the grace to look ashamed, while Scott was filled in with an overview of the rest of the information that he was missing.

"So, outside of the fact that Brody is still lost in the ethers," Scott noted, "what are we doing to find this Iranian group?"

"I've got satellite surveillance on them," Tasha offered. "There is a little bit of traffic, but nothing that really means anything."

"You're still looking at the same location?"

She nodded. "Yes, but from the building across the road."

Scott frowned. "There wasn't a hell of a lot in the way of roads or buildings there, as I recall."

"And there isn't now either," she admitted, "but there is some movement."

"Enough to make you suspicious?"

"Enough that we're keeping an eye on it," Tasha replied. "Honestly, with so many other attacks and killings of anyone we get close to, I haven't really had much chance to do more than keep an eye on this satellite location," she admitted. "I also haven't ID'd any of the people who have gone in or out there."

"But between the drones and the other IT people hired and the gunmen contractors, all out to get us," Wade shared, "we're not short on suspects, except that they're always killed off before we've had a chance to even talk to them."

"That's just crazy," Scott said, "but highly effective at tying up any threads we might have."

"Even the ones we did get a chance to talk to," Damon interrupted, "they didn't know anything. Everybody's been kept away from the bosses."

"Well, that's pretty standard with these guns-for-hire guys to keep them compartmentalized," Scott noted, as he stared at everybody. "So what's up now? Does MI6 have any leads on who attacked Naira at the hospital?"

"I have the video camera footage up right now, and I'm going through it," Sophia shared. "The only person who went into that room was a young woman," she noted, "and you passed her in the hallway."

Scott winced. "Damn. I wondered if that was her," he said. "I got there just minutes too late. We need to find out who that woman is," he snapped.

"I'm on it," Sophia confirmed.

"And the man she met in the hallway," Scott reiterated.

At that, everybody turned and looked at him.

"No man is in the video," Tasha said.

Scott frowned at her. "He met her near the stairway

then. While I watched, they gave each other a kiss, as if he'd been waiting for her."

"Chances are he was waiting for her all right," Terk stated, "but not for the reason that you think."

Scott frowned at that, then got up and walked over and looked at the video. "That's her," he noted harshly, then he tapped the corner of the screen. "He was waiting for her up here."

"So the question really is, was she a part of it, or will we find her body in a dumpster now?" Damon asked.

Scott looked over at his buddy. "Well, I sure as hell hope not. I have a lot of questions I want to ask her."

"Stand in line," Terk said, his voice equally hard. "We've had exactly the same problem every step of the way."

"So, that means they have to be right here in town, following what everybody's doing. No other way they could take out every one of their team members before we do," Scott suggested, his voice hard and angry. "I'm tired of being in defensive mode, it's definitely time to go on the attack."

"You think we haven't tried?" Wade asked bluntly. "Do you think we've been doing nothing but sitting here on our butts, twiddling our thumbs, waiting for another death? We're trying. Believe me," he said, "and it's frustrating as hell. It's not our normal kind of problem, and it even looks like these guys are also trying to take out any women they suspect of having any abilities to keep us alive. So, if they do another attack on us, we won't have them to help us survive."

Scott nodded slowly. "That's what I was wondering about with Naira," he shared. "So you're thinking that's why she was attacked?"

"That's as close as we can figure, unless you've come up

with any other motivation or if she's got enemies you haven't told us about."

"I have no idea on that," he stated bluntly. "I haven't seen her in years."

"And yet when Terk called, she came running," Wade noted.

"Well, we do have a history," Scott admitted. "Not a terribly unusual one, just one full of misunderstandings and mistakes." Scott shrugged. "When she was contacted about me, I think she figured it was her chance at redemption or some bullshit."

"And is it bullshit?" Terk asked him. "Or are you trying to work things out?"

"I don't know where we're at," he said, frustrated. "I never expected to see her again, and, when I woke up from my coma, there she was."

Terk nodded. "And I get that I put you on the spot about it, but I won't apologize. I believe her presence kept you alive, and, if only for that, we owe her."

"I get it." Scott nodded. "Obviously you do what you can for us." Scott ran his fingers through his hair. "But she was attacked twice now, and I can't just sit idly by and do nothing," he cried out.

"Nothing else to do right now," Terk noted. "Sophia's still tracking street cams to see who shot Naira. That will take a while. We brought Naira here where she's safe—or as safe as we can make her for the moment. And whether she believes in what you can do or she believes in what she can do is irrelevant. Whoever it is who's attacking us has probably singled her out because they assume she has abilities, like the rest of us."

"Which is very unfair," Scott snapped.

"Agreed, and we'll do our best to figure this out before somebody else gets killed," Terk stated.

"So, how safe are we here?" Scott asked, looking around. "It's a very odd space for us."

"It is, but it's huge, and we're doing our usual checks and balances, security wise," Terk noted. "But is it 100 percent? No. Nothing ever is."

"Have we had people here? Has the building been breached?"

"Yes," Terk replied. "When they were after Lorelei, someone got in. We are doing everything we can to make sure that doesn't happen again. Everything that matters to us is here, including your partner."

"She's not my partner," Scott snapped.

"Well, she probably would be if you would stop being so damn stubborn about it," Tasha suggested. "Everybody here can see that you two have a very strong connection."

He stared at them, watching as several hid their grins. "Seriously?" he asked in astonishment. "I haven't had anything to do with her in a very long time."

"Yeah, and you've also had nothing to do with anybody else in a very long time, probably because Naira was out there," Tasha noted. "We are all dealing with our histories and the relationships that we had fall apart," she explained, looking over at Damon with a hard look. "We were separated because you guys are natural protectors and felt it was unfair or unsafe for us to be with you, to the detriment of everyone involved, even those who have children," she added.

Scott stared at Tasha. "Children?" At that, Mariana walked into the room. He was quickly introduced to her, but his gaze locked on the little boy in her arms.

"Little Calum," he repeated immediately, and the little boy turned, looked at him, and smiled. "Good God," Scott gasped, suddenly feeling weak at the knees, something he would never have expected. He sat down at the table. "Why?" he asked, looking over at Terk. "Why now, why all this?"

"I'm sorry," Mariana interrupted. "I didn't realize this was a meeting of the team. I'll take Little Calum to our room for a while." The others smiled and waved, as Little Calum was taken away.

"I don't know," Terk admitted. "Maybe it's just time."

"What about MI6?"

"Not only are they barely talking to us," Terk replied, with half a smile, "I think they're trying to figure out how to kick us out of the country." He grimaced at that.

Scott nodded. "I gather there have been lots of bodies."

"Too many," Tasha said, "for all of us. At this point in time we just want this over with, but, in order to have it happen, we need to know who's targeting us."

"You're not getting anywhere on the government leads?" Scott asked her.

"No, they've pretty well locked us out of everything. Lorelei's here," she murmured, nodding to another woman who Scott hadn't recognized until her name was mentioned. "She's technically still working for them, and they think that she's holed up in a hotel, just doing her job remotely. She's tracking as much as she can from the other side."

At that, Gage got up, walked over, kissed Lorelei on the temple. She smiled up at him.

"Hey, if anybody takes a wrong step online within the government," Lorelei declared, "I'll know. The problem is, I'm not sure anybody particularly cares, now that Bob is dead."

Scott's heart failed him. "Bob in the defense department is dead—our boss?"

"Well, yeah, one of our bosses."

He shook his head. "Why is he dead?"

"The murder happened early on, the first one we had learned of, but it's been reported to be a heart attack," Lorelei relayed. "Odds are it was just a case of cleaning up."

"Jesus," Scott said. "Are we thinking he had something to do with this?"

"Or his access gave them what they needed," Lorelei added. "He also had secret detailed files on everyone, with lots of personal information."

"That kind of makes sense," Scott muttered, as he thought about it. "That means this is even more widespread than we thought."

"Not necessarily. All they had to do was take out one person," Terk explained, "and who else would really know about our business, except for all of us?" And he motioned around the room.

"And, of course, everybody who would know is here, right?" Scott asked.

Terk nodded.

"So, we're sitting ducks here. What if they just dropped a bomb on us?" Scott asked in disgust.

"And they could, but no reason for them to do it right now, versus a week or so ago," Terk noted, crossing his arms and leaning against a table.

"Except that now they know that many of us are alive and that what they tried to do has failed."

"Yes, that's right," Terk noted. "We're trying to consider just what the best options are for each of us, but there's no freedom or life after this if we can't put an end to whoever is out to finish us all. Now that they know we survived, the original contract put out on our heads is in default, and somebody is trying to clean up the mess in order to curry favors."

"Of course." Scott nodded. "So we're still not safe, and somebody is still trying to take us out. Even more so now that there's double jeopardy going on, and they might be discovered by their own guys."

"Exactly," Terk agreed, "so we can't have both teams of hitmen upon us at once. The bigger it gets and the more public it becomes, the more danger we are in."

"And there's nobody in the government we can talk to, I presume?" Scott asked.

"They may all think that we're dead, so no," Terk replied.

"So, do they really, or is that all just hidden from them?"

"We were black ops, and there were handlers, who think we're dead," Terk replied. "And, with Bob dead and gone, nobody's there to contradict them."

"Did Bob know any of us survived?"

Terk nodded. "He knew I did."

"Wow." Scott turned to look at the others. "Did anybody else have any communication with Bob after the initial attack on the team?"

They all shook their heads.

"The only one of us who was even conscious at that time was Terk, and he was in bad shape," Damon noted. "I was the first to wake up from my coma, and, since the two of us hooked up, it's been nothing but one fiasco after another."

"And the reality is," Scott surmised, "no way in hell these guys are done. They just attacked Naira hours ago."

"Nope, not done. I agree, and, now that you're on board, you can help us sort it out and get to the bottom of it. It would be great to send somebody over to Iran to check it out, if we could," Terk noted bitterly.

"I was trying to do it long range but couldn't," Damon shared. "We were waiting for Calum to get his strength back and try to get a look over there, and hopefully we can now that we have Rick to ground us."

"How are you doing, Calum?" Scott turned to look at his buddy. "That was always your forte."

"*Was* is the operative word," Cal replied. "I'm definitely getting better, and I'm more than willing to give it a try, but so far nobody's really doing that well with attempts to use their skills in that direction."

"Right." Scott nodded, looking to Terk. "So, who's manning security here?"

"We've got IT markers and our own energy barriers in place and have augmented that with humans on watch on four-hour shifts, which has been working so far."

"Even without a ground?" Scott asked, bewildered.

"It was pretty rough at the beginning," Damon admitted. "But, with Terk's help and now Gage's"—Damon nodded down the hallway—"who is sleeping right now, we've managed to set up something that's been pretty effective."

"Well, that's good to know," Scott stated. "I've been trying to figure out whether or not we are even safe here."

"We've been here for weeks, and, other than the one breach—all three of the intruders dead—there's been no sign of trouble," Tasha noted. "We rescued Mariana and Little Calum from where they were stashed in an unused part of this complex, but her kidnappers apparently didn't know we were right here in another section. I understand that, for you, it may not sound like much, but, for us, after having been under fire every time we go outside, and our attackers being taken out at such an alarming rate, this place is a godsend. I was here from the very beginning, when it was just Terk, Damon, and me, all standing here with nothing. That we now have great equipment, sleeping quarters, a real kitchen, and enough people to rotate shifts is nothing short of amazing."

"Wow, that must have been crazy at the start," Scott murmured. "And it's so great to know that we all have each other's back. The fact that these guys tried to take out all of us at once does sound like a major operation."

"Not only that," Damon murmured, "they even went after our admins. Wilson and Mera were killed. Mera survived the first onslaught but was taken out in a second attack."

"Jesus," Scott gasped. "Even the admins?" He looked over at Tasha. "I don't know why I just assumed that you hadn't been attacked," Scott admitted.

"I was attacked as well," she replied. "Thankfully I woke up in time to get out of bed and hide, so the shots aimed at my bed completely missed me, and the shooter didn't check to confirm. Terk and Damon came looking and brought me in. I've been here ever since. Gradually you guys have come back, and our numbers have doubled, as everyone paired up with their partners."

"And I'm still struggling to sort through that one," Scott shared, realizing how many women were in the room.

"Most of us had some plans in mind for after our retirement," Damon noted, with a bit of humor in his tone. "But apparently we weren't very good about sharing our personal lives and plans with our fellow team members."

Scott shrugged. "I didn't have any plans. So don't lump me into that group."

"Are you sure you weren't planning to go see Naira?"

"No, I wasn't," he stated. "As far as I knew, she was married and off living her own happy life," he muttered. But the idea of checking up on Naira was appealing, and he wondered. "Maybe I would have gotten around to it," he muttered, "once I had some time. I don't know."

"You would have," Terk stated. "Actually I had just sent you an email, letting you know that she was no longer married and hadn't been for a long time."

"And why would you have sent that to me?" Scott stared at his friend in astonishment.

"Because I knew that you needed to resolve that situation, one way or another, in order to go forward with that aspect of your life. It's one of the things that we had talked about."

Scott frowned at that. "I do remember that," he admitted grudgingly. "However, I don't remember giving you the details."

"The details weren't needed," Terk replied, with that same Terk attitude. "I already knew."

"Right." Scott shook his head. "I forgot that that was one of the lessons I was still working on."

"Detachment," Terk said quietly. "Detachment, especially from those who care about us and those we care about. At any sign of conflict, there is always a negative."

"Right." Scott rotated his neck. "There were always those negative aspects to the job."

"Only if you were trying to avoid or to hide from a certain problem," Damon added. "Then it just never got any better. At least not until you were finished doing what you needed to do."

"Well, that's all bullshit," Scott stated, "because it seems like it never got better."

"And I get that," Terk replied, "but, in order to get as calm and as detached as you needed to be, you had to detach from *all* feelings. Whether it was hostility, anger, hurt, pain, or whatever," he added. "In order to fully pull on that energy, you needed to be whole, and you weren't, and that is one of the areas you needed to work on to fully utilize your abilities."

"Right." Scott sighed. "It was always *fun* to do business with Terk." A few chuckles came from the group.

"Hey, I've got my own problems," Terk admitted. "Not the least of which is a woman I don't know who happens to be carrying my child." Terk's voice grew harsher as he spoke. "And she's a continent away. Believe me. If I could be over there and figure that one out, I would, but I'm not. I'm stuck here right now, with the rest of you."

"Time is running out for you on that," Scott reminded Terk. "She won't be pregnant forever."

"She's also injured and has amnesia at the moment."

"Convenient," Scott muttered.

Terk nodded. "Believe me. I've already thought about that. I've also thought that maybe she has nothing to do with this, though I've also wondered if maybe she's behind it." Terk shook his head. "I don't have any knowledge one way or the other."

"Considering how much you know about everything else," Tasha noted, staring at him, "that is pretty unusual."

Terk nodded. "And again, the more I try to force it, the more frustrated I get and the less information I'm able to access."

"Right, back to those same lessons about detachment. Are you sure you don't know who this woman is?" Scott asked curiously.

"No, I have no idea. I've seen a picture of her face, and I don't recognize it."

They all sat in silence for a long moment, stunned.

"Okay, so we still have a lot to sort out," Terk began, returning to the business at hand, "and it's important that we keep the communication flowing to everyone since we have more people now. Basically everybody needs to know everything."

"On that note," Scott added, "you guys need to know that Naira is hoping to leave and to go back to the life that she had before Terk notified her that I was down."

"Well, that can't happen," Tasha said immediately. "We already know for a fact that anybody close to us or connected to us in any way is in danger. Just because she wants to leave doesn't change that."

"I get that," Scott agreed, "but it won't matter. Once she's healed enough to fly, she's pretty adamant."

"Well, then it's your job to make her *un-adamant*," Wade stated, a note of exasperation in his voice. "We've all had to face and to sort out our lovely confusing relationship BS." He faced Scott. "Looks like it's your turn now."

"How the hell does it even come to this? Here I figured I would be single and alone all this time. Now all of a sudden, here she is, just like that." He turned and glared at Terk. "And I do hold you to blame for that."

"Yeah? Well, you can thank me later too," he said, "when you get to the other side of this. I absolutely believe that her presence saved your life. At the moment, you're still hung up on blame," he pointed out. "You need to get past that too."

Scott frowned at him and recognized that everybody else was watching him intently, as if Terk's announcement was supposed to be some kind of solution. "You know that, just because you say something, doesn't make it the law, right?" he asked in a dry tone.

"As you have told me many times before," Terk noted, with half a smile. "And you also realize that just because you try to avoid an issue doesn't mean that the issue will go away, right?"

"Well, it went away for a long time," he noted, with a happy smile. "Maybe it'll do the same now."

At that moment, the door opened, and Naira stepped in. She gasped when she saw how many people were here and quickly took a step back.

Immediately Scott raced to her side. "It's okay. They're all friends."

She looked at him. "I didn't know you had that many friends."

"Neither did I," he said, hearing the laughter of everybody around him. "And some of them are a little more irritating than others."

"Usually"—she smiled at the group staring back at her and Scott—"usually that would make them the closest of friends."

"How do you figure that?" Scott asked.

"Because they're probably only being irritating because they love you."

He snorted at that. "You and Terk can sure come up with the dumbest things to say."

"Which just means you don't want to hear any of it,"

she retorted in exasperation, glaring at him.

"Whatever." Scott raised both hands in surrender. "Let me introduce you to the rest of the crowd. I'm sure you'll get along just fine." And, with that, he introduced her to the rest of the group.

CHAPTER 8

NAIRA SLOWLY SAT down on the chair that Scott had led her to. The pain was just starting to kick in. But then again, she was in this strange and confusing world, filled with so many people she'd never met before. And yet they nearly all appeared to be good friends of Scott's. She was jealous in some ways because they'd had a relationship with Scott over the last few years that she had missed out on. She briefly considered asking Cara if she could help with the pain, but Naira didn't know the woman and definitely didn't trust anything she did at this point either. It was all too weird.

When a cup of coffee was placed in front of her, she looked up gratefully. "Thank you," she murmured. She couldn't even begin to remember what the woman's name was. Luckily it didn't seem to matter.

The woman just smiled at her. "Wow, you look like hell."

"I feel like it too," she murmured.

"Well, it was bad enough getting shot," Scott stated, "but that second attack just wasn't necessary."

"Do you think the first one was?" Naira asked, sending him a sidelong glance.

He grinned. "Well, getting shot is kind of just standard practice around here."

She nodded. "I always wondered just how dangerous

your job was."

"It's not," he stated calmly. "This is a fairly irregular occasion."

She didn't believe him for a moment and knew from the looks of the others that they didn't either.

He shrugged. "It's just something you get used to."

"How? Just how does one get used to being shot?" she asked.

"Well, I can't say that I've been shot very often," he muttered. "And, in this case, I'm very sorry that you were the target."

"I still don't get that," she admitted.

"That's understandable, but I think it's a blanket reaction from our enemy," Terk murmured.

"So," Naira added, "we're back to the idea that you guys and gals all seem to have some special abilities that I know nothing about, and these attackers are afraid that I, by association, may have some too?"

Scott pondered her words and then nodded.

"You know what? That's as good an explanation as any," Terk noted quietly.

"It's really not much of an explanation," Naira said, "as much as a fantastic imagination on somebody's part."

Terk grinned at that. "Well, obviously you don't know all the things that Scott here can do," he replied. "And I presume that's because of all the wonderful history the two of you have perpetrated."

At the term *perpetrated*, Naira's gaze widened. "That's a hell of a word to use." Naira tried to summon up some fighting spirit. Yet all she found was sadness and pain. She shrugged. "Maybe it works. I don't know. It seems all for naught at the moment."

"Well, it depends," said Cara. "I think we all make the decisions in our lives, as best we can at the time. And whether those decisions would have been different, had we had additional information available to us, is definitely a question to consider." She waved a hand in Naira's direction. "But we can't spend our lives racked in guilt because of something we may have done in the past that really doesn't pertain to the future."

"Isn't that like giving yourself a *get out of jail free* card?" Naira asked, with quiet humor.

Cara laughed. "You know what? If that's what you need, that's what you need." She nodded. "I'm all for it. Life is tough enough without us getting completely twisted up over what should have been a simple thing. We all make mistakes, and we all make decisions that would have been different if we had had all the information. That is life."

At that, Naira realized how much she would have changed her life if Scott had said anything at all to her way back then, before her sham of a marriage. She sent Scott a sidelong glance to see him studiously avoiding her.

The others studied them and grinned.

Cara shrugged. "At some point in time, history has to be over, and you must start living for today and not just looking forward to tomorrow either," she noted.

"Oh, I like that," Tasha said, "and I'm in full agreement. I waited a long time for this idiot to have anything to do with me, and the longer we waited, the more unlikely it seemed that it would ever happen."

"And yet," Damon added, "you never said anything to me."

"No," she agreed. "I didn't want to rock the boat."

"That's what I mean," Cara stated. "If you had had other

information, if you had been fully informed, so as to make a fully informed decision, you might have changed your decision way back then. If you'd known that this day would come, you might have been okay to accept that and to wait for him. If you had realized that you could have saved yourself years and years of pain, torment, and self-doubts by approaching him, you probably would have done that too," Cara suggested.

In Naira's mind, it seemed easy in hindsight and ended up being stupid, when hearing that extra bit of information. It was hard to argue with Cara, and Naira wasn't up for arguing. She looked around at the group, as she sipped her coffee. "Well, I get that everybody is aligned for the common good right now." She shrugged. "And I'm sure most of you haven't even determined what you'll do when this is all over with, but it must feel strange to have so many of you here and all in one place."

"Well, it is, and it isn't," Terk replied. "We've worked together as a team for a long time, and obviously we have a few new members added to our original team, but we're adjusting."

"Good," Naira said. "Thank you for giving me a place to stay while I recuperate, but do you have any idea as to who did this?"

"Yes, we sure do," Tasha replied. "Whenever you're ready, I'll show you a video we have from the hospital."

At that, Naira slowly made her way to her feet, then walked over and watched the screen, as it showed the woman approaching her hospital room and going inside. "That was the nurse I saw," she noted.

"Except she's no nurse," Tasha replied.

Naira watched when the woman came back out of her

room, walking calmly, until suddenly Scott appeared in the hallway. She picked up the pace and basically ran to the other end."

"And her running away didn't signal a problem to you?" she asked, turning to him.

"No, because she was running to a man who is outside the view of that clip, just outside the range of the security camera," he explained. "They did a quick lovers embrace, looking as natural as could be, and then they were gone."

"Ah." Naira nodded. "That makes sense then, doesn't it?"

"It makes sense in that she did the job, and he was waiting for her. What we don't know is whether she's a part of all of this or if she was brought into it because of her position at the hospital."

"You said she wasn't a nurse though, right?" Naira asked, looking back at Tasha.

"No, but she is one of the aides who worked the floor," Scott added. "We're still running down hospital credentials, hoping that will give us a clue as to whether she was really part of the system or simply a pawn, but we don't have anything for sure yet."

"It's all just so fantastical to think that somebody went to these lengths trying to take me out," Naira murmured. "Particularly considering that I don't know anything about this."

"The problem is, if they took you out, in the mind of the local police, there would be absolutely no connection to our problems, and, to the killers, it would be a simple, fast job," Scott said.

"Agreed," Naira muttered. "Except for you in the mix, saving me."

Scott shrugged. "You might have survived a little longer. I don't know. You're the one who pulled the needle out of your arm."

"Did I?" She stared at him.

"You did."

"Well, maybe it was pulled out," she suggested, "when I fell from the bed."

"Do you remember falling from the bed?" Terk asked, some intensity to his voice.

She looked at him and shrugged. "I honestly don't remember anything. I do remember that something was wrong with her, that I didn't like something." She frowned. "You know what? I think she said something to me, but ..." Then she winced because her head throbbed. "I really don't know what it was, but I think it surprised me somehow, and, when I reacted, when I pulled out the needle, then she hit me."

"And that would make sense," Terk noted, with a smile. "It makes more sense than you probably realize, and that straightens out the mystery of the needle and the head blow."

"Yeah." Naira nodded. "That would explain some of it. Yet I really don't know what she said to me."

"It doesn't matter now," Terk noted. "You'll remember it eventually."

She wasn't so sure about that but was more than happy to have the pressure off her to try and sort it out. As she sat here and watched the security video once more, she shook her head. "It still seems a little odd."

"Maybe not." Terk's phone rang just then. He answered it. "Go ahead, Merk. I'm putting you on Speaker."

"Have you got Naira?" he asked, his voice tense.

"We do. She's right here with us."

"Good," Merk replied, "because the woman in the video

clip from the hospital was found in the hospital dumpster this morning. Her head had been bashed in."

SCOTT HEARD THE news like a gut punch to his solar plexus. But the shocked gasp from Naira brought him to her side. "It's okay."

She stared up at him, her bottom lip trembling. "How can you say that?" she cried out. "That poor woman."

And he realized that it wasn't fear for her own safety that Naira felt but shock and sorrow for the other woman, even though she had tried to hurt Naira. He sighed. "Look. I know it seems terrible and outrageous and so many other things, but, when you get in with the wrong crowd—and in this case any association appears to be the wrong crowd—it seems that, as soon as someone is involved, and they mess up, they are out. And"—he pointed—"they're out permanently."

"And how is it that she messed up?" Naira asked, staring at Scott in shock.

"Chances are it's because she didn't get the needle job done properly, and she had to hit you over the head—which completely changed whatever their plan was. Also they would consider her job completely messed up because you managed to leave the hospital alive and well. That kind of failure is not something these people would have tolerated."

"Do you think she thought it was a failure?"

"No, she probably didn't know at all what was coming for her," Scott explained. "I suspect that some male deliberately seduced her, befriended her, whatever you want to call it, then convinced her to do this, either as a part of a job or out of love." Scott paused. "There are any number of reasons why somebody would get sucked into doing something like this. And when she didn't do the job properly, she was taken out. That way she can't talk, and honestly, given that she was probably led in this direction right from the beginning, there was a very good chance she would have been taken out anyway, even if she had succeeded with her job. Apparently that's been the way this whole scheme has been going."

Naira stared at him in shock, realizing what kind of world he lived in. "Good God," she whispered. "She wasn't very old."

"No, she wasn't."

"And she was really pretty," she murmured. "Why would she even get involved in something like this?"

"I'm guessing her lover probably came across as her Prince Charming," Scott replied.

Naira winced. "Wow, women can be really pathetic sometimes, can't they?"

At that, Cara reached across and gently patted Naira's hand. "We tend to be, yes, but not forever. We do come to our own senses, as we grow older and get a little experience in the world."

Scott realized that the women already had some rapport that he didn't understand—and probably didn't want to either. He took a tentative step backward and looked over at the others. "So, she's been taken out. What do you think their next move is?"

"Wade is on watch at the moment," Terk noted in a harsh voice. "So you're safe here, Naira."

"I would presume that the only thing they can do is come back around after us," Scott suggested.

"Do they know where we are?" Naira asked.

"I don't think they do. Otherwise they would have already attacked us here," Terk replied.

"And what about your brother?" Scott asked.

"His safety is always a concern, and he would never lead anybody back here. In fact, Merk and I rarely see each other," Terk noted, "but Merk is pretty wily."

"Sure, but nobody is wily forever," Naira added, inserting herself into the conversation. She shot Terk a look, making Scott chuckle. "And, if he's involved, you know they'll be after him."

"And I can tell him until I'm blue in the face to be careful, and he would tell me that he's fine."

"But he's not fine," Naira argued irrepressibly. "You should bring him in here."

"Well, I would if I could," Terk agreed, with half a smile, "but you don't know my brother."

She frowned at him. "No, but I'd like to, and, in order for that to happen, he has to survive."

At that, Terk burst out laughing. "I'll tell him that you're concerned."

"He doesn't know me from Adam," Naira replied in a dark voice, "but I don't want him to die. Sounds like there have been far too many deaths over this nightmare."

"I agree with you totally," Terk said in a mild voice, as he studied her. "Turn your attention to Scott and keep him safe," he suggested. "As we know, your connection already works for you."

"What's the point?" she asked, turning and glaring at Scott. "He won't listen anyway."

Scott's eyebrows popped up, and he stared at her. "You don't know that."

She snorted. "Of course I do. You never listen to anybody."

He flushed, feeling all gazes in the room on him. "That's hardly fair," he noted.

She just gave him a hard look, making him realize just how much they still had to discuss.

"Obviously we've still got some discussions to have," he said to the others, "but I would like to get back to sorting out a solution to our current problem." He waved his arms around this place. "With all of us gathered here, are we not all just sitting ducks?"

"We are in a way," Lorelei replied.

At that, Mariana walked in again, Little Calum in her arms. "Is it okay if we join everyone?" She smiled and walked over to Calum, who immediately held out his arms for his son. The boy dumped himself sideways, so he could be caught by his father, with laughter in his voice. Calum held him up. "There's trouble," he murmured, as he tossed him in the air. The little boy laughed and laughed, and Calum grinned.

"I don't know what to say, Calum," Scott said to his buddy. "I didn't see this coming. This isn't what I thought your life outside of the team would look like."

"Nope, neither did I," Cal agreed, "but I've got to tell you. It's a hell of a lot better than what I ever imagined it to be." At that, he added, "Here she is, the best answer I could have hoped for," he stated calmly, as Mariana walked over, and he tucked her up close. "I made the mistake of keeping them away, trying to keep them safe. And you know what? They got kidnapped anyway. We had a really close call, all of us, and life feels mighty fragile right now. We need to quit wasting time and pushing away our loved ones in the name of 'protecting them' and start enjoying the people we love," he murmured, then gave Mariana and Little Calum a squeeze.

Scott had a lot to think about. Not the least of which was the woman at his side. He was still stunned at seeing how many couples had formed in the few weeks that he'd been unconscious. And maybe coupling up in bad times was a good thing; he didn't know, but it was definitely fascinating to see the results. And, for that, well, he was happy for all his friends.

CHAPTER 9

SEVERAL HOURS LATER, after another nap and during a meal, Naira verbalized the thoughts that were in the back of her head. "Given that everybody here is wanted by whatever enemies you guys have apparently amassed, why don't you use this facility to our advantage and set it up as a trap?"

Silence followed, as several people put down their forks and looked around at the others.

"I've been thinking about it," Terk confirmed, "but certain dangers are inherent in that."

"Of course," Naira agreed. "Clearly Mariana and Little Calum would need to leave."

At that, Mariana shook her head. "I can tell you that's not happening," she stated. "I risked a lot to get here, and I'm not interested in leaving."

"I understand that," Naira replied. "However, if things are going down, you can't help because you'll be looking after Little Calum. So maybe it's best that you're not here while it's happening."

Mariana looked at her. "And, of course, you'll leave too?"

"I'm not sure I can leave," Naira said. "Apparently I'm still on the hit list."

"Everybody is," Terk stated. "And it's not a case of you

being on the hit list or not. It's just that you're associated with us. And, yes, obviously we would ensure that all members of the team were safe, before something like setting a trap could happen." He smiled at her. "It's a discussion to be had with the whole team."

She nodded. "And yet I think they would defer to you."

"It's not a case of deferring, Naira," Terk explained calmly. "We are a team. Therefore, we are here for each other."

"Which really just means that nobody will make a decision because they're waiting for you to do it."

He gave a bark of laughter at that. "And you've only just arrived," Terk noted. "How do you figure that?"

"Because you're the boss," she stated calmly, "even though you say it's a team."

"She's right," Damon said, before Terk could really say much more. "We are a team, but you're definitely at the helm."

Terk glared at him, but Damon just smiled back, unrepentant. "Whether you like it or not, boss, it's always been you. All you."

"You're right. I don't like it," Terk shared. "I have enough on my plate."

"Yes, and you'll head to Texas pretty damn soon," Damon added.

Terk nodded grimly. "Yes, but I can't leave you guys."

"Which means you have to solve this first," Naira said calmly. At that, he glared at her again. She shrugged. "I get that you can kill with that look of yours, but it's really not helpful right now."

"What are you suggesting?" he asked.

"Whenever someone goes out for supplies again," she

offered, leaning back, "set a trap."

"That could be very dangerous," he murmured. "Everybody here could die."

"Everybody here could die at any point in time already, as we have found out. These enemies don't appear to have any scruples as to what they're planning on doing."

"I think annihilation is their number one plan." Terk stared at her in fascination. "Why would you want to put yourself in that position?"

"Because I want a life after this," she shared, "and this is not living."

Terk chuckled. "I don't know about *not living*, but it's definitely a different kind of living."

"It's not living," she repeated firmly. "We can't just hide away because somebody's after us. I understand that works for a little while, but it doesn't work anymore. And somebody has to help the one missing—Brody was it? And you need to go to Texas for whatever reason," she said, with a wave of her hand. "So all these other people are waiting for things to be done."

"I agree." Tasha nodded. "I know Naira doesn't understand the whole scenario here, but I think she's right. This isn't living, and we can't keep this up indefinitely. We have more people now, and they are getting stronger every day. We have done all kinds of missions in secrecy and set up all kinds of operations. I think we should try that here."

Terk was quiet for a moment, then he spoke. "I'm not sure it's time yet."

"Why not?"

He took a long deep breath. "Because of Brody." The men all exchanged hard glances.

"Okay," Naira added, "so I don't understand who this

Brody is, and why you can't set a trap without him."

"That's because you don't necessarily understand the type of work that these guys do," Tasha guessed. "And I'm probably not the one to tell you, but I'll give you the short and simple version."

By the time she'd finished talking, all Naira could do was stare at her in shock. "You're serious?"

"Very serious." Tasha nodded.

"Which is why I've been trying to keep you out of all this," Scott murmured beside her.

She stared at him, frowning. "And you never told me after all these years?"

"Back then I'd never really defined my skills," he noted. "There were just things I could do, but I didn't really tell anyone. Only since I started working with Terk here have I managed to develop them on a completely different level."

Naira stared at Terk. "So this is something that you've always been able to do?"

He shrugged. "Since I was little, yes."

"And your brother?" she asked.

"He says no," Terk replied.

"He says no," she repeated, slowly questioning him. "You don't appear to be very convinced of that."

"I'm not sure that I'm convinced or not," Terk replied. "However, if my brother says that he doesn't have these abilities, I believe him."

She stared at him. "That's BS."

Terk burst out laughing, while the others just stared at her in shock.

"That's an odd way to talk to Terk," Scott noted.

"That's because you guys have worked with him for years, have respect for him," she noted bluntly. "I barely even know him. He brought me over to help with you," she murmured. "But at no time did I feel like he was concerned about me. His concern was all about you."

Scott winced at that. "Terk is very protective. So, when he knew I was in trouble, he did everything he could to balance things in my favor."

"Right," she agreed. "That's what I mean now. I know that whatever he'll do will be good for him and for you guys, but that doesn't mean it'll necessarily be good for me."

When a long silence followed, she knew she'd shocked them. She continued to play with her fork, while she waited for somebody to speak up. They all looked at each other, as if to figure out who would handle this.

Mariana was laughing now and spoke first. "Looks like you did something that I didn't think was possible. You stunned them into silence."

"I like to call a spade a spade," Naira replied succinctly.

"You're quite right," Mariana stated. "I never had any doubts that Terk was committed to the safety of his men. … And because that means he's on the same journey as I am— as in I want to keep my beloved alive and well too—I didn't have any argument with it. Now I presume the reason that you are having trouble with this is because, from your perspective, it appears to be your life on the line, yet nobody cares."

She shrugged. "It's not that nobody cares," she explained carefully. "Obviously I'm here and not still at the hospital, where I was attacked. Since I'm not a part of the team, like you are, I'm just not sure that the end goal is one that's in my best interests."

"And that's what's really important, isn't it?" Terk asked quietly, studying her, an odd look in his eyes.

She frowned. "No, not necessarily. But having survived two attempts on my life, I would like to keep surviving."

He nodded. "Of course you would. It's just interesting to find out that you believe that I would somehow rank your survival not as important as somebody else's."

She smiled. "I think when you love, you love deeply. And when you hate, you hate equally deeply. As for the space in between, you feel ambivalence."

Terk's eyes widened. "Interesting. You could be right." He shrugged. "There are only so many things in this world I can completely drive myself crazy over." He shook his head. "And that may not be a bad assessment of it."

Naira sighed. "Right or wrong, even if you guys survive this and do well, I would like a life again," she stated. "There's no guarantee that I'll get out of this alive at all, and, the longer we sit and wait, it all becomes more difficult. The worse the tension will get, the worse supplying a group this size will get, the harder to disguise our existence here will be. It just seems to me like things need to be brought to a head, one way or another."

"Absolutely," Terk admitted. "I agree, but it has to be done safely."

"Of course. Obviously we want to maximize the odds of however many people survive."

"No," Terk stated adamantly, "we ensure that *everyone* survives."

She raised an eyebrow, as she heard his tone and the truth in it. Then she settled back. "Maybe, but that's really the first time I've heard that sentiment from you, that conviction for what the goal is here."

He smiled. "And you and I haven't talked very much, so I can understand how you wouldn't know who I am on the inside."

She frowned, as she looked at him. "Oh, I think I know who you are," she declared boldly. "At least I understand what kind of a man you are, and that says a lot. I have absolutely no doubt that every person in this room, outside of me, is incredibly important to you. If for no other reason than the health of your own friends, I think the guilt of anything happening to them would tear you apart."

He nodded. "That's quite true," he murmured, "particularly if I put together an operation with too much haste, and it ultimately fails."

"Got it," she noted. "And if you keep Scott alive, then, as you well know, that's a large part of my battle."

"Hey, enough of that," Scott protested beside her. "I told you that I don't need any help from you. It's just put a target on your back."

"Yeah, well, you're full of BS too," she exclaimed, looking at him. "Terk's right. I came over to help you."

SCOTT FOUND IT odd to hear Naira speak of herself like that. It was also even odder to hear her speak about him. Scott hadn't had anything to do with the decision to bring her here. It would have been his last choice, if he'd had the opportunity to be asked about it, but Terk had gone ahead and spoken to Naira, knowing that it would have been for the one reason she had stated, and that was to keep Scott alive.

Maybe it was well past time that he stopped fooling himself about what he and Naira meant to each other. It might help her find some peace with the situation she was in too.

He looked over at Terk. "I think she has a point though."

Terk nodded. "She does, indeed, but it has to be something that we set up properly. And we can't have Brody being a victim of it all."

"Can someone explain how it would put Brody at risk when he's not even here and isn't even conscious?" Naira asked. She was obviously still upset, and likely stunned, by the news that Tasha had shared.

"Because Terk's helping him," Scott added.

"Not just Terk but Cara as well," Mariana noted.

And, with that, Scott looked over at Cara. "I'm not sure that we've formally met before, although I remember you from my time in the coma," Scott said, "but thank you for helping Brody."

"You're welcome," she murmured, "although I'm not sure how much help I've been. I was initially brought on board to help Rick." She shrugged when Scott stared at her in surprise. "Terk tried to recruit me a long time ago, and I declined."

"Sounds like that's been our loss," Scott murmured.

She smiled. "Well, I'm here for the team for now. The future remains to be seen."

Scott nodded. "Sounds like you and Rick have worked out some kind of a relationship."

"I'm not sure *worked out* is quite the right answer," Cara shared. "Let's just say that we're connected, and it's a work in progress."

Rick laughed. "That's one way to put it. When Cara saved me, she did so by going to a very deep energy-level work to keep me alive. I can't say I really appreciated it once I learned, but she did. I didn't necessarily understand either, and I certainly didn't know that, when I came back out of my coma, a bond had been forged, something I couldn't break in a million years."

Cara looked over at him and smiled. "I told you to disconnect further if you wanted to."

"Only if you promise to chase me down again," he replied.

Scott realized that Cara's and Rick's energy bond had gone so much deeper than even Scott knew was possible. He frowned and looked down at his hands. It was almost embarrassing to see something so intimate and clearly so special. As Scott turned to Damon, Scott noted Damon looking at Tasha too, acknowledging their own energy bond.

What had happened to this team? They'd all become paired up while Scott had been unconscious, and it just made his current situation with Naira all the more pointless. He'd always loved her, so was it finally time to revisit that whole scenario and see if being together was what they wanted? He faced her. "I suggest we go have a talk."

"Well, *you* can talk." She yawned. "However, it's time for my medicine, and I need to crash."

He watched in concern as she slowly got up, her movements awkward, knowing that sitting for too long was taxing her system. Plus he realized how much being around all these couples who had worked out all their own problems was having an effect on her emotions too. He rose and said, "Come on. Let's get you back to bed."

She moved out with a goodbye wave to the rest of the group and headed toward her room. Once inside, she stated, "Don't worry about me. Go on back to your friends. I'm sure I'll be just fine."

"I'm sure you would be," Scott replied, "but I'm staying." When she frowned at him, he shooed her to the bed and added, "Don't even bother arguing. Go take your painkillers and crash."

The fact that she walked to the bed without a word, reached for her pills and the water on her bedside table, swallowing them in one gulp, revealed the level of fatigue she felt. When she carefully lay down, he watched as shudders rippled through her body. "You know you didn't have to stay that whole time."

"But I wanted to," she murmured. "It seems like everybody here is so capable, so in control of who they are, and, despite the current obstacles before them, they know where they are going. I felt like a fish out of water, but it was so fascinating that I didn't want to leave. I was probably way too harsh on your friends. I'm sorry about that." With a shrug, she tried unsuccessfully to pull the covers over her shoulders.

He quickly walked over, grabbed the blanket, and gently wrapped it high around her. "Here," he murmured. "Let somebody help you for once."

She didn't say anything and just closed her eyes. Yet her words had already relayed a lot. As a matter of fact, they spoke volumes about her own insecurities.

But why wouldn't she feel insecure? It's not like any of this was easy on her. It wasn't easy on any of them, but she'd come into it without knowing anybody; plus she was already hurt, frightened, and under emotional strain. So, of course, she wasn't feeling very well overall.

He sighed, as he sat down beside her. "We can work this out, you know?"

"You've already worked it out," she murmured. "Just go take care of your life. I'll be just fine."

"You *are* my life," he declared in a harsh voice, getting

pissed off at her attempt to send him away.

She smirked. "Yeah, sure. Tell me another one. I'm too tired to argue with you. Just go."

"Maybe if you're too tired to argue," he quipped, "you'll listen for once."

She opened her eyes and glared at him. "This really isn't good for my attempt at healing."

The thing was, she was right, and that just pissed him off even more. "Well, you already hate me," he snapped, "so you might as well hate me some more."

She frowned at him. "You're not making any sense."

"Maybe not," he admitted, "but neither are you."

"Fine, you can go ahead and talk, but that doesn't mean I'll listen."

"You'll listen," he said in a hard, tight voice, "because I've had enough of this." She just shrugged and then shuddered. Immediately he felt like a heel. "And why are you fighting me? You should be here trying to heal us."

"*We're* trying to heal?" she cried out. "I don't want to be here. I wanted to go to a hotel, where I was on my own, in my own space, on my own turf."

"Nobody would consider being in a hotel as your own turf," he argued in frustration.

She glared at him. "Yet I wouldn't be sitting here with all these people who are your friends," she snapped. "People who seem to be in the know about things I can't even begin to understand."

Scott nodded. "I get that it's probably frustrating that you were out of the loop, but it's not as if I was in any position to bring you in. We haven't even had a loop between us in a very long time."

"So you say," she murmured.

"Why did you come when Terk contacted you?"

"You *know* why I came." And then the tears started. "And for the dumbest reason of all."

"What's that?"

"Because I love you," she snapped. "Because I always have loved you. Because I was sorry I did what I did, and I hated myself for it, but I felt like I had to go through with it. I've been miserable every damn day of my life since then, and I'm sure you are thrilled to hear that too." And then the hot tears fell, unabated.

And he felt even worse; yet, at the same time, her words had the effect of something like a chain releasing within him. "Why the hell didn't you say that when you first got here?" he roared, as he glared at her.

She stared at him. "Say what?"

"That you still love me."

"I never stopped loving you, you idiot," she cried out. "Why would I have even come if I didn't?"

And he realized just how much he'd been so determined to not see that. That he'd been blinded to that. Rather than giving her a chance to argue, he gently lay beside her and pulled her into his arms.

She protested, "Just leave me alone."

"I'm afraid the window for that has passed," he murmured against her hair.

When she broke into deep heavy ugly sobs, his heart broke, and he felt terrible that he'd been a part of this sorrow in any way. He just held her for a long moment, rocking her gently back and forth. "God, I'm sorry," he whispered. "I'm so sorry." It seemed like nothing would stop her sobbing, and he started to worry about her getting even more ill from it.

He held her close, rubbing her back, stroking her hair, smoothing her hair off her face, murmuring, "Calm down. Please just stop crying," he whispered. "You'll make yourself sicker." Finally she wore down and was brokenly sobbing in his arms. He held her close and whispered, "I promise that it'll get better."

She gave a broken sob. "It'll never get better. I never should have come here."

"If you hadn't come," Scott replied, "I might not even be here right now."

"And, as I now know, that's just bullshit," she murmured. "I'm sure Terk could have brought you back out alive without any problem."

The crux of the matter was that she felt used. As if everybody else knew what was going on, but she didn't. She'd come over in good faith and was the only one who wasn't part of the team.

He held her close and said, "What you don't understand is that Terk is already helping Brody on an energy level. Terk's energy is already keeping security on this place, and his energy has been supporting the rest of us for weeks, while unconscious and now conscious. Terk's energy has been stretched *very* thin for a long time. He never would have had you come, except he needed your help," Scott murmured. "And so did I."

She calmed down and was still tucked up against him, although she wasn't saying anything. He would give her a little bit longer to calm down, and then he wanted to have a heart-to-heart over this whole thing. Yet, when he looked down at her, she was almost asleep again. "Go to sleep now," he murmured. "It's fine. You're safe, and I'll be here when you wake up."

"No, you won't," she disagreed, her tone soft and so sad that it broke his heart. "You'll be off in whatever life you've chosen for yourself with your friends, and it doesn't include me."

"Well, it could," he noted, "if you're prepared for the life of an energy worker. I can't guarantee our safety, especially not right now. But this is my life, and I can't really change it."

"You mean, you don't want to change it."

"I don't think I can anymore," he murmured. "I don't think you realize just how much my abilities make this the proper place for me."

"I still don't even understand these abilities you all speak of." She shifted her head, so she could look up at him. "I never heard about them before."

"And I get that," he replied. "I really do, and I'm sorry because maybe we should have talked about it."

"You think?" she asked in jest.

"But I didn't think you'd believe me. And honestly, at that point in time, I hadn't really developed enough to really understand it myself. We haven't seen each other in a very long time."

"I know," she said, "and I guess that's why I thought maybe you would have forgotten me or at least forgiven me in the meantime."

"I should have," he admitted. "Terk has told me that I needed to deal with issues in my life in order for my abilities to really come on stronger, and that this avoidance was holding me back, but I kept telling him to butt out, to get out of my life, and to stay out."

She snorted. "I owe him more than I realize then because obviously he was right."

"And he is right. Unfortunately that's something about Terk. He's nearly always right."

"That must get damn irritating."

"It does. And now he has his own problems, but he knows we all love and support him."

"And he's trying to get to Texas?"

"Yes, he's trying to get to Texas but doesn't dare go until we get this situation resolved. I can only tell you the little bit I know, but what I tell you, you must keep in confidence. Please." And he explained about Celia.

By the time he was done, Naira was sitting on his lap, staring at him in shock. "Oh my God," she whispered. "Why would somebody do that to her?"

"We don't know, and Terk doesn't even know who she is."

She shook her head at that. "Wow, he really does have problems."

"More than you can imagine," Scott stated, "but his first priorities are right here with us and with the team."

"And with Brody," she added, with a nod. "I'm understanding that a little bit more."

"Terk won't leave Brody alone, and he's the only one still out in the ethers, and he hasn't had the benefit of everybody's help to get back on his feet. Terk is desperate to make sure that Brody comes back too."

"Of course," Naira agreed, with a heavy sigh. "He's part of the team. For the first time, I realize what it's like to have a team. Honestly I'm kind of jealous."

"And that's where you need to stop because, of all those women out there, the only one who worked directly with us was Tasha. We had two other admins—Wilson and Mera— who worked with Tasha initially but were killed in this entire mess, and Tasha nearly was," Scott explained. "They were taken out almost at the very beginning of the attacks on our team."

Naira grimaced and shook her head. "You really need to get these assholes."

"We really do," he agreed, with a nod, "and I'm glad you understand that because you're right. Life won't be the same until we can get this situation stopped."

"Not just stopping it." She frowned, looking at him. "You have to go beyond stopping it. You have to make sure that nobody ever gets a chance to do this again."

"Which is why we also need Brody back—to ensure he doesn't get hurt in the process. So Terk has to stay safe and apparently Cara too," he added darkly, "because it sounds like she can do some serious energy work too." He shrugged. "I really don't know because I've never even heard of her before now."

"All these talented women," Naira murmured, "make me feel like shit."

"Well, it shouldn't," he disagreed, "because that's absolutely not what we're all about here."

She smiled. "Maybe not, but that doesn't help much with my self-esteem."

He shook his head. "What I need from you is some acceptance that things between us can get better, and they will. We just need a little time to sort through everything."

"It depends on whether we'll get that time," she murmured. "The minute somebody comes in and starts firing, you know we'll all be the targets."

"Yes," he agreed. "I get that. I'm just hoping we can keep you alive through all this."

"Me too, but it's not looking very good," she murmured. "Not looking very good at all."

CHAPTER 10

W HEN NAIRA WOKE, it was dark, and she was alone. Memories of the conversation with Scott filtered through her mind. Had he really said all that? Had he really made it clear that maybe it was time for the two of them?

She wasn't at all sure about that. Some of their latest conversation was drifting back and forth in a hazy drug-induced memory. When the door opened, she shifted, so she could watch as Scott came in quietly.

"Are you awake?" he murmured.

"I think so." She yawned. "I feel like shit though."

"Of course you do." He walked over, bent down, and kissed her gently on the forehead.

She frowned at that. It was definitely new, but she'd take it.

"All forgiven?" he asked.

"I'm not even sure," she admitted. "So much of whatever conversation we had is a haze."

"Hopefully not all of it," he teased lightly.

She shrugged. "I don't know. Depends if we talked out all our differences or not."

"Not all of them, I'm sure," he replied, "but most of them, yes."

"You want to give me the CliffsNotes's version then?" she asked in a dry tone.

He sat down and searched her face intently. "Seriously?"

She shrugged. "I guess I don't really remember everything very clearly."

"That's fine," Scott said, "as long as you remember enough, and we'll work through the rest."

"Work through?"

"Yes," he repeated, "we'll keep you alive through this whole mess, then see what comes of our world afterward."

She frowned. "I heard something in there about all that, but I don't think I got that level of clarity from my memories."

He smiled. "I promised I'll try to be good and help you remember as we go on."

"If you say so." She yawned again.

"Can you go back to sleep?" he asked, with a frown. "If you're that tired, maybe you should."

"It's not even a case of tired as much as it's just not feeling quite awake yet," she murmured.

"I'll go get you a cup of coffee," he offered. "That might help." She watched as he disappeared again, and she smiled. Maybe it would be a good day after all. She wasn't too sure where they were at right now, and she would have to clarify it when he came back, but maybe, just maybe, they had a chance.

When he returned with a cup of coffee a few minutes later, she was sitting up against the headboard of the bed and rubbing her scalp.

"Are you all right?" he asked.

She nodded. "I'm fine. At least I will be when I get some caffeine," she replied, with a more cheerful tone than even she expected, once Scott handed her the cup of hot coffee. She was still very wary, not exactly sure that they had resolved everything between them, but he seemed to even get that too.

"As we take our relationship step by step, don't worry about it," he suggested.

She frowned. "It's hard not to. I'm not exactly sure where we stand."

"We stand wherever we want to," he murmured. "However, we're definitely in a whole lot better place than where we were before."

"Says you," she muttered. "Somehow it doesn't feel that way." She blew on her coffee to cool it a bit.

He grinned. "Last night it felt that way," he stated, "so I won't let this morning and a little bit of brain fog set you on a different path."

She snorted at that. "I'm glad you think so because, right about now, I'm not at all sure."

"You will be," he noted. "You're just feeling a little insecure."

"Of course I am," she muttered.

He nodded. "But you came to look after me, and now I'll look after you."

"Out of guilt?" she questioned.

"No," he said, "because I care. Remember that."

She frowned, really wishing she had a better idea where they stood but was willing to go along with it. "So does this mean I'm not leaving right now?"

He laughed. "No, you sure aren't, but I do want to get you out of this room—or at least out of bed, if you don't need to be in one," he corrected. "We're making plans to try to locate Brody on the ethers."

She stared at him with wide eyes. "I do remember part of *that* conversation," she noted, "and somewhere along the line, that's when I started to lose it."

He smiled. "And you can be expected to have some confusion over all that." She winced and put her hand to her head. "Is the headache still bad?"

"No, it's much better," she admitted, dropping her hand. "Sleep helped. I just was checking the bandage."

"Good. As soon as you're ready," he said, "get up and get dressed, and we'll continue the conversation out there with the others."

"Did my bags come with me?" she asked, looking around.

He nodded. "They did arrive from the hotel, but I don't see them here. Let me go find them." And, with that, he disappeared again.

She wondered if a shower was asking too much. It would definitely be on her wish list to get one. She wasn't sure if Scott would throw a fit over it though, what with her wounds bandaged up. So she waited until he returned with her bags. "Do you mind if I have a shower?" she asked.

He looked at her with an assessing gaze. "What did the doc say about getting your wounds wet?"

She shrugged. "You'll have to ask me about that later. I'm having severe brain fog right now."

"I'm sure a shower would make you feel a lot better, wouldn't it?"

She nodded.

"How about we see how you feel when you get up on your feet again," he suggested.

She put down her coffee cup and carefully got up and then smiled. "You know what? I don't feel half bad. My head feels a lot better." She reached up a hand to the bandage and winced. "Getting rid of the stickiness and the dried blood would help a lot too."

"I agree," he murmured. "Do you want me to stick around while you shower?"

She frowned and then shook her head. "No, I'll be fine." She didn't really want him here, watching to see how she made out.

He gave her another long assessing gaze and then nodded. "Fine, but you call out if you need me."

She laughed. "I won't need you."

He smiled at her. "And, even if you did, you wouldn't let me know, right?" he teased. And, with that, he was gone.

She wondered if it would always be that way between them. As if they each knew each other so well, yet, at the same time, not very well at all. He was right; she was stubborn that way and did not like to ask for help if she didn't need it. But sometimes you just needed that extra bit of support from someone. Finishing her coffee, she made her way to the bathroom and stepped into a hot shower. As she made her way under the showerhead, it was amazing to just stand here and have the warm water wash over her.

It was almost addictive. She made a slow process of first removing the two gauze bandages. Naira was certain a first aid kit was around here, and she could have someone put two new bandages on her wounds. Then she worked at the blood still in her hair, just getting the strands of hair wet first, then slowly adding shampoo and letting it soak in before she gave it a gentle scrub.

By the time she was done, she felt so much better and not even horribly tired. The bullet wound felt so much better as well. She let the soapy water trickle over it, trying to make sure she didn't injure it while cleaning her hair, but it seemed to have done the job quite nicely.

As she returned to the bedroom, she found the clothes and her backpack she'd traveled with and got dressed. With that much under her belt, she picked up her cup of coffee again and finished it off. And then she slowly walked out to the other room. When she got there, the room was full of people. She winced again. "Wow. It'll take me a while to remember all the names."

At that, the woman she remembered as Tasha stepped up. "Don't worry about it," she said. "You'll figure us out pretty fast. How about some coffee?"

"I'd love one," she replied, looking around, finding a little coffee station off to the side. "I can get it," she protested.

Tasha waved her hand. "I'm sure you could, but, right now, you are injured, and we don't want you doing too much. So I certainly don't have a problem getting you a cup," she explained. "How is the head? Do you need new bandages after your shower?"

"I probably do need new bandages. I'll have Scott fix me up later. However, while the head's been better, it's much better than it was last night," she murmured.

"Good, that's what we want to hear."

Naira laughed. "You sound like a bit of a cheerleader."

"Yep, I sure am," Tasha agreed. "And I'm always rooting for the home team."

Was there any warning in that, or was Naira just being overly sensitive? She didn't know anymore. By the time she'd gone through her second cup of coffee, she almost felt normal. Then her stomach started to growl. She winced and looked over at Scott. "I hate to ask, but any chance of getting something to eat?"

"Absolutely," he replied. "What sounds good? We can

do the whole cereal thing, bagels, or we could cook some eggs. You probably could use some protein."

"Eggs would always be my preference," she admitted. "But, if nobody else is eating right now, cereal would be nice and easy."

"Eggs are fine," he said. "I was just waiting for you to get up anyway."

"You could have woken me," she protested.

He looked at her and shook his head. "Now why would I do that? You're hurt, and we're trying to let you rest and sleep as long as you need to get you back on your feet."

She frowned because she didn't want to appear to be a burden among this strong and confident group of people.

"Don't even start thinking like that," Scott said, as if reading her mind.

"What?" she asked. "I'm not allowed to think now?" But her tone was dry, and everybody laughed.

He grinned at her. "That's better. A little bit of humor goes a long way."

"But just a little bit, right?" And then she laughed. "I do feel better today, and I'm sorry if I was a little harsh last night." She turned around to face Terk.

He looked at her in surprise. "Honest suggestions and truth are never wrong here," he stated. "We are not such delicate wallflowers that we have to worry that our every word might upset someone here."

"Good," Naira replied. "In that case I won't worry."

He smiled. "Good. I will try to be nice to you for a little bit," Terk said, with a hint of a smile, "but, after that, the same goes."

She nodded, then chuckled. "Same goes, I hear," she murmured.

Just as Scott set a plate of eggs in front of her, a series of alarms went off. Her heart froze, and she looked around, as everybody bolted into action, except for Scott. He sat down beside her, his gaze attentive on everyone else.

"What's wrong?" she asked in a hoarse whisper.

"Somebody has triggered something we're monitoring," he explained. "I'm not exactly sure what the setup is here. Although I've been working at getting up to speed, I'm definitely not quite there yet."

She frowned at that. "The alarm bells don't sound good."

"Sometimes it sounds worse than it is." He watched and waited until things calmed down, and then Terk walked over and sat down beside him. Scott asked him, "What was that alarm about?"

"Somebody on the perimeter." Terk frowned.

"Someone prepping for an attack maybe?" Scott asked. "At least definitely testing our boundaries."

"Yes. I'm assuming that we were … you were," he corrected, "followed here."

"Bullshit." Scott stared at his friend. "I sure as hell hope not."

"In a way," Naira murmured, "it would be the best thing."

Terk nodded. "It would, but again other people are involved."

"I get that. I really do, but trying to find a solution to this means bringing it to a head."

Terk smiled. "You have a bloodthirsty way about you," he noted. "I like it."

She laughed. "You have no idea," she murmured. "Trying to get things sorted in my life has been a little bit on the bloodthirsty side all along."

Terk nodded. "It's never as easy as we might like to think it is," he noted, "and it doesn't happen as nicely as we would like it."

She smiled. "No, you're right there. I was hoping that we would be a little farther along than we are."

"I think you're doing just fine," Scott murmured. "And, by the time we're done and have our plans set up, you should be good to go."

"Good to go where though?" she asked.

"Nowhere, of course," Scott replied, with a wry smile.

She looked over at him. "So what am I supposed to do? Just move here and live in this compound?"

"Yeah. So were you working before?"

She nodded.

"A graphic designer still?"

She frowned and then nodded.

"I didn't know if you were still working while you were married."

"Even more then," she noted, "but, yes, I have my own business, and, yes, it is mobile."

"Graphic designer," he murmured. "Do you still keep up with your artwork?"

"Not very much." She shrugged. "I just haven't felt like it lately."

"Maybe it's a good time to reinvest in you."

She laughed. "You mean in *you*?" Her answer startled him, and he broke into a laugh. But it was one of the first really free laughs she'd heard out of him this whole time.

"Maybe." He looked at her. "But what I meant was that you are one hell of an artist, and it would be a shame to lose that."

"I don't know about losing it, but I have to be in the right mind-set." She shrugged again. "I can't say that I've been there for a while." He nodded and didn't say any more. She looked over at him. "How long do you think I'll be staying here? You don't have any long-term plans here anyway, do you?"

"Nobody has any long-term plans right now," Terk interjected immediately. "We're all focused on getting everybody through this."

"Agreed." She nodded. "And I'm sorry. I'm not trying to push. This is an interesting time, where no one really has plans, so I can't make plans either."

"Exactly," Terk noted. "Sometimes it's okay to live in the moment."

Her lips twitched. "Does that work for you?"

"Lots of times, yes, it does," he confirmed, with a serious attitude. "It's all about what you make of it."

"Well, that would be nice, but I don't know about the *what we make of it* part," she murmured. "I can't say that I've had a chance to do much along that line in a very long time."

"If you want any artist supplies while you're recovering, let us know," Terk stated.

Scott nodded. "The injury is on your left side, and you are right-handed. So we'll see what we can figure out."

She looked at him, frowning. "It seems odd to start something like that in the middle of all this."

"Yes," Scott noted, "it may feel that way, but, if you don't start, you're only pushing off until tomorrow something that maybe you're better off starting today."

She frowned at that logic because it would mean really relaxing and settling in—into her artwork and into this place. She wasn't sure she could do something like that yet.

But he was right, and it might even be better if she was stuck here for a while. She frowned and let out a long breath. "I'll think about it."

"Do that," Terk agreed cheerfully. "Now I think Little Calum over there would love someone to play with."

The toddler sat on a chair at the kitchen table, entertaining himself with Play-Doh.

"Cooking a meal for us?" she asked Terk.

He winced. "As long as whatever he has there won't be for me, I don't care. He's happy, and he's having fun. Considering how little we have to keep him calm and quiet around here," Terk noted, "that hasn't been an easy challenge for Mariana."

"No, of course not," Naira agreed. "I might help a little later, as I heal a bit more," she suggested. "I'm just not sure I'm necessarily up for that level of noise right now."

"If you ever want to read a story to the child, Little Calum is one serious bookworm," Terk noted.

"Not to mention an artist in the making," she noted, as she watched him slap his hands into the clay or whatever it was he was playing with, making weird shapes and then mashing it down flat again. "And he's fast," she added. "You've got to love that."

Terk smiled. "And he's happy, so everybody's good with it."

"I can imagine," she murmured. It couldn't be easy being here, with everybody thrown together, yet being on their own, each with their own mess, trying to figure out what was happening in their lives. Naira wasn't a big help either, but she wouldn't go there; she had enough on her plate to worry about right now.

She watched as everyone seemed to have something to

do. She couldn't imagine what she could ever do in this scenario that would be of any assistance to the team. She looked over at Terk. "This whole alarm thing doesn't bother you?"

"It's why we have the warning systems up," Terk explained. "If we didn't have it, I'd be worried because I'd be wondering what our enemies were up to that I wasn't aware of."

"What does this actually tell you?"

He looked at her with respect in his eyes. "See? Those are the kinds of questions that we need to ask. What it tells me is that somebody is wandering around outside, within the designated perimeter, as if looking for where we might be."

"But you don't know whether it is the enemy or some citizen out for a walk, correct?" Naira asked.

"No, that's exactly right," Terk replied, with a smile. "We don't know if it's any issue at all. What we do know," he murmured, "is that somebody is out there."

She frowned. "So, did somebody go out there to look?"

"We have it on satellite, so they're checking right now."

When Tasha joined them, she smiled. "It looks to be a false alarm."

"But how would you know for sure?" Naira asked her. "Do you keep track of people who have been here in our area before, like those who have walked around outside?"

"Exactly," she noted, "and we have confirmed somebody is out there, a male. He isn't acting suspiciously, but we will keep an eye on him. However, this is not somebody we have seen here before."

Naira frowned. "So, to me, that seems like more than a false alarm."

"Why's that?" Tasha asked.

"Because you would think they would send somebody new every time. And, if that's the case, this is your new one." She stared at Tasha soberly.

"That's a valid point," Tasha said. "I'm not saying it isn't somebody we should be aware of, just that it's somebody we haven't had so far."

"Agreed," Naira noted. "This must be a fast-moving event for you guys."

"It happens a lot, being on a public street and all," Tasha murmured, "but not a whole lot we can do about the foot traffic."

"No, so I guess the task is to register how many people come, how often they come, whether they come in waves or come in a pattern."

"And we are doing that," Tasha confirmed, "but it's interesting that you would say that."

"Why?" Naira asked.

"There's just enough going on that we aren't sure what is happening, so we're doing exactly what you said. We're keeping an eye on it. It seems like whoever it is will send various people at various times, just to see what they can learn."

"Exactly."

"Anytime you want to take a look at the security screens," Terk told Naira, "you're welcome to."

"What would that tell us?" she asked him curiously.

"We don't know if it's someone you might have seen somewhere, like at the hospital."

She frowned and immediately but slowly got up on her feet. "Let's go take a look."

With Scott, Terk, and Tasha at her side, Naira headed over, until she stood in front of the screens.

The monitors were huge, and Sophia had backed everything up, so Naira could take a closer look. When they got to the man who had just approached, causing the alarm, she sucked in her breath. "He's one of the men at the hospital, one of the orderlies," she said, gasping in shock. "You know what? I just … When you said that I might recognize our visitor, I wasn't even thinking it was a possibility. Yet there he is." Naira's stomach began to revolt. "Now I feel sick," she murmured.

"No being sick around here," Tasha declared, eyeing Naira carefully. "Definitely not near the equipment."

Naira laughed. "I didn't mean it literally."

"Good, but I did," Tasha stated. "This equipment is pretty sensitive, so no getting sick on it."

"Got it," Naira noted, with a smile. "Let's see the rest of it."

They watched as the man took a casual look around.

"And right there. Is he taking a picture?"

At that, Sophia leaned forward. "You're right. I didn't catch that. It was very subtle. Wait. … Look how he's using his hands, as if to signal something or someone."

"That's very interesting," Naira said, as she stood here, watching it run again.

Scott put his arm around her. "That is why we insisted on you being here," he explained, "so we can keep an eye on you."

"It's definitely unnerving to see somebody from the hospital here, after I've been attacked at the hospital."

"It is, and that's why you're here instead of alone in a hotel room somewhere," he reminded her.

She glared at him. "But then the danger wouldn't have come to everybody else," she noted, as she pointed to the room around them. "Now everybody's in danger because of me."

"No. Not because of you," Terk corrected. "We're all in the same danger because of whatever started this whole mess in the first place. All these other issues and attacks ultimately happened because the original attack—intended to take us all out—failed," he stated. "You are in danger because of us, not the other way around."

She waved her hand. "You're splitting hairs."

"Not at all," he argued. "Regardless, we have enough to worry about without assigning blame."

She nodded. "I agree with you there," she said, "and we definitely need to do something to make sure this guy doesn't know we're in here."

"We're working on that," Sophia shared. "As you can see, he's wandering around, but he doesn't have a direction to go to. He's—"

"It's almost like a fishing expedition," Naira guessed, interrupting.

"That's exactly what it is," Terk agreed. "He's looking for any outlet, any explanation of where we might be, but he can't figure it out. That is because we have an energy guard up, and the building itself isn't exactly welcoming. He can't see a door, so, as he continues to walk around, it'll look like it's some sort of a secure facility, which is not necessarily something we want him to find out already."

"I wouldn't want him to find it out at all," Naira replied, "because, the more suspicious it is, you know it'll make him want to find answers. And eventually he'll find them. It's just a matter of how quickly it happens," she murmured.

Terk smiled at her. "And I know you don't realize this because it's all new to you. However, this scenario, … all of it and far more, … it's what we do."

She frowned as she looked at him. "Meaning, I can just sit back and trust you?" she asked in a dry tone.

"Don't ever do that if it doesn't feel right," Terk stated, his tone so serious that she realized he meant it. "It is always critically important to follow your own instincts. And now that you've ID'd this person, we do understand that he's still looking for a way inside."

"Of course he is. I mean, anybody who thinks we're here will try to get inside, won't they?"

"Yes, absolutely," Scott confirmed. "And the fact that you could ID him is perfect."

"So, with that double confirmation," Terk added, "we'll have to take some action."

"What does that mean?" Naira asked in alarm. "I really don't want to get involved in murders."

He looked at her and then chuckled. "So what then? Murder is okay, as long as they only kill you or us?"

She frowned at that. "I guess that was a pretty stupid statement, wasn't it?" she admitted grudgingly.

"No, it was honest," Terk said, "and I'm glad to see that you have a strong sense of ethics."

"Oh, I would like to think so," she replied. "I'm just unsure where all this is leading. But obviously we have to solve it so these guys stop. What is it they're after?"

"Annihilation," Scott stated succinctly. "The complete and perfect annihilation … of all of us."

"Everybody here, including you," Terk told Naira. Then he turned to look at her, just as he was about to walk away. "So, how do you feel about murder now?"

SCOTT HELD NAIRA close. "Terk didn't mean it that way."

"Of course he did," she argued, then smiled. "I'm not innocent of the ways of the world. Obviously I don't want to contemplate anybody getting hurt, but, if it'll be either them or us, I choose them. I have too much to live for."

Scott reached down and gave her a big kiss.

She smiled and cuddled closer. She wasn't even sure that they were exactly where they needed to be, but she was willing to go the distance to find out. As she looked over at the others, all smiled at each other. Whatever else was going on, they appeared to be happy about the situation between her and Scott. He walked her back over to the kitchen table.

"Do you want to just sit down and rest a bit now?"

"I feel like I've done nothing but rest," she mumbled. "Is there anything I can do?"

"Not when you're injured," he said cheerfully.

She glared at him. "I'm hardly injured," she replied.

"What would you call it?" he asked her, with interest.

"That's a trick question," she muttered. "I know you too well to fall for that." He burst out laughing, swept her up into a careful hug, and held her close. "This is definitely a change for you. You're much happier, more lighthearted."

"It is a change for me," Scott admitted, "and I am happier. I'm not sure how we got to where we were, but I'm sure happy with where we are now."

"Me too," she said. "I just wish I remembered all of that conversation."

"You will," he replied instantly.

She frowned at that. "Says you."

He grinned. "I forgot just how contrary you like to be."

She sighed. "Not really, definitely not, but you know what? At some point in time, you just have to give up the ghost and stop fighting."

"Don't ever do that," he said. "It's beautiful to have such spirit." She looked at him sideways. He grinned. "See? You've got that look on your face that says you don't believe me."

"I *don't* believe you," she confirmed, "and it makes it a little hard to trust you completely."

"Come on," he coaxed her. "You're doing just fine. Don't worry about it."

She smiled. "How about I still worry about it, but I'll try to keep it under control?"

He laughed at that. "Good enough."

She looked over to see Sophia eyeing her with an assessing gaze. Naira walked closer. "Is there anything I can do to help?"

Sophia studied her and asked, "Are you any good with computers?"

"Yeah, no," Naira admitted.

"Any good with IT at all?"

"No," she repeated.

"Then you can't help me," Sophia declared. "But you know what? If you're up for searching the kitchen for cookies, a little man over there really could use one."

As Naira turned to look, Little Calum watched her hopefully. "Cookies?" he asked, and such hope filled his voice that everybody stopped to look at Naira.

She smiled, automatically glancing over at Mariana expectantly. Little Calum's mother gave her the okay, with a nod and a smile.

"Why not? Raiding a kitchen is something I definitely know how to do," she murmured. She looked back at Terk from across the room. "This doesn't mean I can get banished to the kitchen all the time though."

He looked at her and shook his head. "Never, that's not my style. Never go to the kitchen unless that's where you want to be."

She faced the little boy again and said, "Let's do it." Then, with her mind on making herself useful and with Little Calum in tow, she headed for the kitchen.

As Scott watched her progress, he smiled to himself.

Tasha walked over, gave him a quick hug. "Glad to see things are getting better."

"Well, we're getting there," he shared, "but she's got a way to go to trust me yet."

"Of course she does. She's had some shocks to her system, in addition to the injuries," she murmured. "It won't be resolved easily."

"Sure would be nice if it were," Scott said, with a heavy sigh. "It seems like the shit's always hitting the fan around us."

"It probably will be for a while to come too," Tasha noted. "At least until we get this thing solved."

"Yeah, you're right about that."

"So, you did recognize this guy from the hospital?"

He nodded. "Absolutely. She's right. He was at the hospital with her. I'm kicking myself for not looking at the video as soon as you guys got it."

"Enough of that. So he's with them at the hospital, casing her. What I find interesting," Tasha added, "is how they even knew about her."

"The only thing I can think of," Terk suggested, as he came up alongside them, "is that they had been following me. And, from me, they found her. The problem with that is, if they found her, have they also found Brody?"

"We'll have to make sure that doesn't happen," Scott noted. Then he frowned. "I might as well tell you that, while I'm getting stronger every day, I'm definitely not back to full speed."

"Nope, you're not," Terk agreed, with a smile. "But, if it makes you feel any better, you're not alone. And just like the others, you're making steady progress. So we'll take it and be damn happy."

"I get that," Scott noted. "I just wish I was stronger and could do more."

"What you can do is stay strong, so that none of this keeps blowing up in our face. Because, when these guys make their attack and stretch their wings to do whatever it is they're planning on doing," Terk suggested, "we'll need all hands on deck. And hopefully that'll be you too."

Scott wanted so badly to be back to normal, to be strong enough to be a solid help. The last thing he wanted was to bring the two of them here to the temporary headquarters, only to be a burden on everyone else on the team. It's not the way Scott functioned, and of course the team knew that, but it still wasn't enough to make him feel comfortable with the situation.

He needed to pull his own weight and be even more proactive than that. But he was also still unclear as to what he was supposed to be doing right now. As he turned toward the kitchen, he saw Naira, nodding off in place.

He winced, then got up and walked over to where she and Little Calum were sharing a plate of cookies.

"*Shh,*" he whispered to the boy, his finger to his lips. "I'll bet Sophia and Tasha might want a cookie too," Scott said softly. With that, Little Calum grabbed a handful of cookies in each pudgy hand and headed for the control room, a big smile on his face. Then Scott moved next to Naira, and he gently nudged her. She jerked and cried out at the pain of her sudden movement. He crouched down in front of her. "Hey, let's get you back to bed."

She stared at him with pain-filled eyes, clearly confused, and he realized her body had a lot more healing to do. "Come on," he said. "Also time for pain meds."

"I sure won't say no to that," she murmured, as she slowly stood. "I didn't realize I was nodding off. How embarrassing."

"Well, you were," he stated cheerfully, "and this isn't where you need to be right now."

"Says you," she muttered, as her gaze moved to the plate of cookies. "Oh my gosh, where's Little Calum?"

"I sent him off with cookies for Sophia and Tasha, so he's fine," Scott replied, helping her to her feet. "Right now, let's get you back to bed. You've got a lot more healing to do."

She sighed. "Why does that sound like it'll take a whole lot more time than I expected?"

"It probably will," he admitted. "Absolutely no way to know."

She groaned. "I really don't like the sound of that."

He easily led her back to the bedroom, where he got her settled on the bed, flat on her back. "Let me change those bandages and give you your medicine."

"I really don't feel so good," she murmured but laid down as he worked on her.

"Exactly my point. No need to put on a bright face in front of everyone on top of everything else you're going through," he said, his voice gentle. "Everybody will still be there when you're feeling better."

She looked at him, blurry-eyed. "It just feels like we should be doing something."

"The trouble is, all the guys were injured, some badly," he reminded her, "and we're all coming back. While it may seem like we're okay by looking at us, the reality is, those special abilities we have are something that we count on when the going gets tough, and that is what we're having the most trouble getting back in a way that is proficient and reliable."

She sighed. "I'm a case in point too, aren't I?"

"Maybe so," he agreed, "but making sure you stay safe is the most important thing. And we don't want anybody else getting hurt."

"It would be nice if I was the last one attacked," she said, and then a big yawn took over, making it hard for her to talk.

He smiled, grabbed her blanket, and tucked her in. "Just rest," he murmured. "That's the only thing you need to worry about right now. Just rest."

She nodded and sank into the pillows. "Wake me up for dinner, okay?"

"Sure," he asked. "Are you hungry?"

"Well, no, I had cookies with Little Calum," she replied, with half a smile. "But any time I get hurt or even sick, I tend to get really hungry as I heal."

"That's good to know," Scott noted. "I'll take that as a positive sign then."

She would have smiled, at least he figured she would have, but no way to get her lips to move at this point. She was already out and snoring gently.

He smiled as he quietly closed the door and headed back to the main room. The others looked at him. He nodded.

"She's out cold already."

"Good," Terk replied. "It's always worse when they fight it."

"She doesn't know what she's fighting though," Scott reminded him.

Terk nodded. "Of course not. More to the point, in her mind, she's still fighting the person who attacked her."

"And waiting for all this to be resolved," Tasha added faintly. "She's right in many ways, like her suggestion that we should set up a trap and lead them here."

"Well, it looks like they've already found us," Terk noted, "so what we need to do is fortify for the coming attack. We must ensure that whoever needs to get out," he added, with a look over at Calum, "gets out safely."

Calum winced. "You know Mariana won't like that."

"Maybe not, but, if she knows an attack is imminent, I'm sure she won't have a problem taking Little Calum somewhere safe."

Cal nodded. "I can try, but you know that she's also fairly stubborn." At that, the others just smiled.

"Sounds like a match made in heaven," Sophia teased.

Calum groaned. "Hey, I'm not stubborn."

"No, not at *all*," she said, with a chuckle. "You are absolutely not in any way stubborn." He just glared at her. She smiled. "I'm trying to be honest," she added, "but you're not letting me."

Cal sighed. "Fine. … I'll talk to her tonight."

"You do that," Terk said, "and we need to get everyone on board here and set up some perimeter defenses."

"What exactly do you want to do?" Scott asked Terk.

"The same as we did in Iran," he noted.

They all stopped and stared at him.

"What do you mean?" Lorelei asked.

"You heard me," Terk stated. "We had quite a system there, and it's what the team knows. Our enemies may not," Terk noted, "but I think it would work well right now. And I don't think they would expect it."

"Yes, but, if that's what worked well for us," Tasha asked, "don't you think they would have studied this method in the meantime?"

"I don't think many people in that group are left," Terk noted. "So, no, I don't think that will be an issue."

They sat down together and got to work on their plans.

Scott listened and agreed with almost everything that was planned. "I still think we need to remove as many people from here as we can," he shared. "Maybe using that as a way to draw them in, thinking we are down to a smaller staff or something."

Terk looked at him, considering the suggestion. "I presume you're talking about moving out women and children."

Scott nodded. "Absolutely, even if they have been through a lot," he added, "they don't need to go through more."

"Presumably you're talking about Naira right now, but have you considered the fact that she may refuse?" Terk asked him.

"Sure," Scott agreed, "and I fully expect her to refuse, but I don't want it to be something that we have to discuss. This needs to be a decision that we make based on what's right for the group, and everybody needs to fall into line, whether they agree or not."

Terk agreed. "I'm just not sure how you guys will handle it."

"That's our problem," Wade noted calmly, as he looked

over at Sophia.

She snorted. "In your dreams."

"You heard Terk," Scott protested.

"I'm a part of this team," Sophia stated, "and I'll be here monitoring who's coming and who's not coming and don't even begin to try to talk me out of it."

Wade looked over at Terk, who shrugged. "She's got a point. We'll still need the team here."

"Which is why I'll be staying too," Tasha declared. "That makes sense. We're part of the original team, and you need us. We're operatives."

"As for the other women, they're not," Sophia said, "and while they have great things they can do for us, it may not be the time to be putting people who don't understand how we operate in the midst of an attack."

At that, Terk turned to Scott. "See what I mean?"

"I see what you mean," Scott admitted, "and this will be a bigger problem than anything."

"And it could be," Terk agreed. "Definitely something that we have to find our way around."

Scott shook his head. "I don't know. I suspect, if one gets to stay, they all want to stay."

Mariana spoke up, having stepped in moments before. "Not necessarily," she replied. "Each of our situations are different. In my case, I can't help you, and you won't need food, so I can leave you more than enough supplies prepared," she added. "It's not like this will be for very long, and you don't need me and Little Calum here giving you something else to worry about."

"Thank you," Cal said, with a smile, looking relieved. "I would feel much better if you two weren't here." She gave him a look. "For your own safety," he added, turning up his palms.

"And I understand that," she replied, smiling, "but not everybody will. Little Calum makes our situation different."

Cal nodded. "I get that too. I expect there will be some upset people, and I'll be sorry about that, but I still think we need to do whatever is right for the group."

"I understand," Mariana said, with a smile, "but that doesn't mean that everyone will let you off the hook quite so easily."

He groaned, rolled his eyes, and agreed. "No, they won't. That's just a given."

She laughed. "As long as you have some patience and tolerance, I think they might surprise you."

He looked at her hopefully. "You think so?"

"Well, I hope so," she said, "but no guarantees."

Scott figured that, if it were a majority decision, it would be a lot easier for individual partners to leave. Especially if they knew that they weren't the only ones who were being shown the door. He had to agree about Tasha. He would have expected her to stay anyway. That just made it more difficult of course. He added, "Let's get as many plans made as we can. We don't have much time."

At that, they turned toward Terk.

Terk spoke in a low voice. "Are you forgetting something?"

Scott looked at him. "You know something? I am." He frowned and added, "I'll need a few minutes to figure it out."

Terk nodded. "Take what time you need. Meanwhile, we'll put more plans into motion." And, with that, he gathered up the rest of the men and took off for a war room meeting, while Cal sat here and stared at Scott.

"Are you sure?" Cal asked Scott.

"No, man, I'm not sure," Scott admitted, "but something definitely doesn't feel right."

"That I can believe. Nothing really feels right anymore," Calum agreed.

"It's just kind of bizarre how this all works out—or doesn't," Scott noted. "Yet I think they somehow have an idea that we are here."

"Well, if they've had any way to track us, they've tracked us here. They just don't know whether we're inside or not," Tasha guessed.

Sophia spoke up. "The guy in the video bent down and picked up something off the concrete. That might have confirmed it for them somehow."

Scott asked, "Can I see that video?"

Sophia brought it up, and Scott walked over and took a look. He winced. "There." He pointed. "I think that's Naira's hair clip. I noticed it dangling, but, at the time, getting her inside and to bed was all I was thinking about. Damn."

"Well, it looks as if she may have lost it, and that's all they needed for confirmation," Sophia noted.

"All they needed to know that we were here somewhere." Scott cursed. "I didn't need to give them any more details than that."

Tasha interrupted. "We know that members of their group, now deceased, knew we were here, or at least nearby. Mariana even had a tracker embedded in her neck when we rescued her from her kidnappers. And they came after Lorelei with the noise machine inside this very room, so finding a hair clip today doesn't really even matter now."

"We're also all running on the assumption that somebody in that enemy group has energy skills," Sophia noted.

"And, if that's the case, maybe that's all they needed."

Scott had to agree with that. "It will be more than a little upsetting if that is what's going on," he said. "We've been pretty complacent about our enemy, thinking only we had this level of abilities."

Tasha smiled, nodded. "You're not the only one to bring that up," she murmured. "But, at the end of the day, we have to set all that aside, work together, and do the best we can, with what intel we have at the time."

CHAPTER 11

WHEN NAIRA WOKE, she lay in bed quietly and assessed the damage. She felt pretty decent. Her stomach growled, but then—depending on what time it was and whether they had yet to wake her for dinner—she may have slept through the night. Her bedroom had no windows, so she'd have to ask someone.

She almost felt a grogginess of having had too much sleep.

When the door opened a moment later, and Scott walked in with coffee, she looked up at him. "So, is that a peace offering?"

He stopped in surprise. "I don't know," he hedged. "Do I need one? A peace offering, I mean?"

"That depends on whether you let me sleep through dinner," she complained. "Is it the next morning or still later last night?" And then her stomach growled yet again.

"Morning. I figured you needed the sleep to best help you with the healing." His eyebrows popped up. "You really are hungry, aren't you?"

"I was hungry before I fell asleep last night," she stated, all the while looking at him through narrowed eyes.

"Sure, but I wasn't really aware that it was this level of hunger."

She shrugged. "It's pretty normal for me."

"Good enough," he replied. "We do have fresh muffins. Let me go grab you one, or I'll make that two." And, with that, he was gone before she had a chance to say anything.

Muffins would be great. Anything to help take that edge off her hunger that was beginning to be problematic, at least as far as her angry stomach was concerned.

When he returned a few minutes later, she sat up and shifted once again, leaning against the headboard, holding the coffee cup with both hands. Her eyes lit up at the two large muffins he brought.

"Now that," she said, "I can get behind." He walked over and handed the plate to her. She immediately started munching away, not even waiting for her coffee to cool. By the time it was cool enough to have a drink, she was ready to wash down some of the muffin. As soon as the first one was gone, she held back on the second one.

He looked at her and asked, "Too much?"

She shook her head. "No. I'm just trying to give my stomach a moment to remember what food's all about."

He groaned. "It's not that bad."

She grinned. "Feels like it though. So, what did you guys decide?" she asked.

He frowned and asked her, "What do you mean?"

"When I was chased off to bed," she said, "I'm pretty sure you guys wanted to make some final decisions on what we're doing."

He nodded slowly. "Yes, and no," he murmured.

"So, am I being sent away?" He nodded, remaining silent, as if waiting for a big blast from her. But she was well past the point of blasting. "Good," she agreed. "I presume some of the other women and certainly Little Calum are leaving too."

"Some of them," he noted cautiously, as if surprised.

She nodded. "The ones I expect to be leaving would be Mariana and Little Calum. But since Lorelei has CIA clearance and skill, plus Cara has her *skills*, those two would stay maybe?"

He nodded. "I think that's probably a good bet. Cara is still working on Brody, and she's working to get Rick back up to speed. He isn't quite there yet, and neither am I, for that matter," Scott admitted.

"So, *of course* you'll leave too then," she replied smoothly. He just looked at her. She laughed. "Of course not."

He added, "The people who are involved are the ones who are part of the original team. Everybody else will be moved out."

She stared at him. "So, how do you think moving us out will work?" she asked curiously.

He shrugged. "Well, let's just say we're hoping it will work."

She smiled. "I'm sure you are, and also I'm sure an awful lot of things can go wrong."

"Absolutely," he agreed. "And we're really trying hard to make sure that nothing does."

She glanced around the room. "It's funny because you're really close to having everything set up here, aren't you?"

"Yes, though I'm not sure this is where anybody particularly wants to stay."

She nodded. "More plans to sort out for when this is over."

"Exactly," he murmured, "and something else for you to think about too."

"And what's that?"

"In case I don't leave the industry," he noted, staring at

her intently.

She frowned, tilted her head. "Meaning, am I okay with you going out into this dangerous field every day, leaving me to wonder if you're ever coming back?"

He slowly nodded. "Yes. … This is what I do. It's what I've always done."

He had stated it so simply, but also so much else was going on in the background that she knew he was just giving her a simplified version of it. "Well," she replied, "if it's that versus not seeing you anymore, I guess it's that."

He continued to study her steadily.

"Don't worry. I can trust that you'll do a good job and that you'll do the best you can at keeping yourself safe," she said. "At one point in time, we *all* have to cross that great divide, but I'd like to see you not do it anytime soon."

"Agreed," he noted, with half a smile. "However, there is absolutely no guarantee in life."

"You know that yourself, since I could easily have been killed twice in the last few days. You would have been racked with guilt over it," she stated, "but there wasn't a way to stop the attacks—at least I lived through both. Obviously we're all aware that there is a certain level of danger, and we'll do the best we can to avoid having any of it coming down on our heads."

"That's true enough," he replied, with feeling. "However, I think you're wrong about not having anything we can do about it. We're all trying."

"Of course you are. I didn't mean it like that. I was just thinking that we would all be in the same boat, with everybody trying to protect everybody else. And I don't want to see me protected over anybody else," she added, with a wave of her hand. "I'm probably not explaining it very well, but I just think that there is room here for everyone to stay safe. And that just means cooperating and acknowledging that the danger will be ever present, while you guys carry out these operations. At some point in time, hopefully before you get old and gray and too slow for that one bullet that's got your name on it"—she grimaced—"you'll retire."

He stared at her in fascination for a long moment, then nodded. "That's the plan."

She smiled. "And we know what they say about best-laid plans."

He grinned. "We sure do. At the same time, you really sound like you've adjusted yourself to some of this."

"Well, I'll put a brave face on it, and I will adjust to it as time goes on," she replied, "because the other option is not having you in my life." At that, tears threatened to choke her throat and to run down her cheeks. She shook her head and cleared her throat. "And that," she stated, "is something I don't want to happen. The last few years have been very miserable without you."

He walked over, sat down on the edge of the bed, and just held her close. "Not just for you," he murmured. "I was probably taking too many chances on jobs because I didn't really care, because I knew I had nobody to come home to," he murmured. "And it wasn't a good attitude, but some of the guys said things about me being a little bit too ..." He stopped, then frowned.

"Maybe not careless but ambivalent?" she asked.

"Yeah, something like that," he noted, with half a smile. "Just know that I will be much more careful from here on out."

She smiled. "You do that. You look after you, while I do my best to look after me. ... I'm not exactly sure what I'll do for a living if we're staying here in Manchester, but I presume I can find something to keep me busy."

He laughed. "I'm sure you can. And, if nothing else, I'm serious about you focusing on your art again."

She frowned, then considered it for a moment. "I don't know." She shook her head. "I seriously haven't done any painting since … you know."

"Since what?" She just looked at him. His eyebrows shot up. "Since we split?"

She nodded. "How could I?" she murmured. "It was all part of the same thing. You were my creative freedom, and, when I lost that, out of guilt, more or less"—she shrugged—"I couldn't do my art anymore. So maybe you're right. Maybe it is time I get back into that. … Maybe when this is over."

"Definitely when this is over." He laughed. "No maybes on that front. And now, are you ready to get up?"

She winced. "If I must."

"I'm just not sure how you're feeling and whether we need to look after you a little bit better."

"No, I'm good."

He smiled. "You don't always have to be the tough one, you know?"

"Funny, I thought that was your thing."

He grinned. "Sometimes it is. Sometimes it definitely feels like it too. And other times, well, it'll be whatever we can make it."

She gave him a bright smile. "Now, if you'll give me a few minutes, I'll get up and get ready." Then she stopped and asked, "Am I leaving now?"

He hesitated, and then he nodded slowly.

She winced. "So soon?"

He nodded again.

"Is the attack imminent?"

Again he nodded, very slowly this time.

"Well, shit." She stared at him, not sure what she was even supposed to say. "Do I have time for a shower?"

He hesitated. "How about a short one?"

At that, she shook her head. "In that case, I'll skip the shower and get dressed. It won't take me a minute to pack up my things."

"It's already packed up."

She turned and gave him a flat stare. "Is everybody out there waiting for me to wake up?"

"Maybe." And then his grin picked up. "Don't forget that you are hurt and get some leeway."

"Good Lord, I don't need any leeway. I just needed a chance to sleep."

"Well, you got it," he replied cheerfully. "And now? Well, now it's time to get up."

SCOTT WAITED OUTSIDE Naira's bedroom door until she opened it up and poked out her head. She looked at him and frowned. "Have you been standing there, waiting for me?"

He nodded. "Are you ready?"

"I guess, not that I have much."

"Well, that's a good thing right now." Scott stepped inside, grabbed her bags, and said, "Let's go."

She followed him without asking any questions, and, for that, he was grateful. There was a time for questions, and there was a time for action. She seemed to have gotten that down pat, and he appreciated it. There would be time for talking later. He led her out into the multiple-car garage and helped her into a large SUV.

She looked at him, silent until he went to close the door. "Remember what you promised me," she said.

He smiled and nodded. "I remember." And just as he went to close the door again, she stopped and leaned over with her arms open. He immediately wrapped her up and held her and whispered against her ear, "Honest, you'll see me again. I promise."

"I will," she confirmed, with a nod. "I'm holding you to it." And, with that, she sat back in her seat and buckled up. She looked over to see that Calum was driving. "How did you become the designated driver?"

"The family," he replied succinctly.

And she winced at that because it made sense. She took a look around to see that almost everybody was here, with only Sophia and Tasha having stayed behind. Naira looked surprised to see Cara with them. "I guess with your skills, you can work remotely?" At Cara's nod, Naira asked her, "Are you okay?"

Cara gave her a one-arm shrug and then smiled and said, "Yes, more or less."

With that, Naira nodded. "I think that probably describes all of us, doesn't it?"

"It does right now, I would think."

And, with that, Calum drove out of the large building.

Naira looked at him. "I don't suppose we have bullet-proof glass, do we?"

"Actually we do," Cal confirmed.

She stared at him in shock, then settled back into her seat. "Well, that's good. I'm glad you guys value your cargo."

"There's nothing more valuable than what we have

here," Cal noted. "And, as much as I wanted to stay behind with my team, believe me. I understand what needs to happen here."

"Not to mention, you're still injured," Naira pointed out. He glared at her, but she grinned. "I just thought I'd bring that up."

"You don't need to," he muttered. "I'm very aware."

"He's also trying to convince me that he'll return to the compound, after we are stashed somewhere safe," Mariana murmured.

"Isn't that what you wanted?" Cal asked Mariana.

"Sure," she replied, "but the chances of you coming back after going to the compound are pretty slim. I just didn't want you to think that I wasn't aware of that."

He shook his head. "We could all just get along for now."

"We could," she noted cheerfully. "And you know something? It probably will happen, but it might not be today."

CHAPTER 12

S ENSING UNDERCURRENTS, NAIRA looked around and asked, "Are people really against us all to that degree?"

Mariana sighed. "Obviously none of us are particularly happy to be targets, but I need to take our son somewhere safe."

"Exactly," Calum muttered.

"And for some of us," Cara added, "I would work better if I'm not under fire."

Naira stared at her. "You know what? One of these days I would really like to know what you mean by *work better*."

Cara looked at Naira, surprised, then shrugged. "You won't like it."

"You don't know," Naira noted. "Maybe I will."

"Well, we'll see. I suspect we'll have some time to kill at the new place."

But her phrasing made Naira wince. "I would prefer a completely different term or phrase for that," she noted.

"Wouldn't that be nice," Mariana muttered.

"Of course I didn't mean it that way," Cara replied, looking at both of them. "I'm just saying that we'll probably have some time before there's an actual attack."

"Any extra time is a good thing," Calum stated. "We need a chance to set up better."

"Yeah, I can see that," Cara agreed.

"And some people, like Scott, aren't fully healed," Naira reminded them.

"That's one of the reasons why I need to be in a better place," Cara noted, "so I can help."

Naira stared at Cara, realizing what she was saying, and added, "It must be nice to have those kinds of skills."

"It's nice, but it's also not so nice," she murmured. "I can't save everybody."

Naira wasn't sure if that was a warning, but it almost sounded like it. She glanced around and saw that everyone appeared to be in a pensive mood. Of course they were. They were leaving behind their partners. She looked back at the compound, but it was hard to see. "Is it hard to see because we're so far away or because somebody's put up some kind of a barrier?"

Calum laughed. "Both. The barriers are very important right now."

She nodded. "Of course they are. It's just kind of bizarre seeing it firsthand."

"All of this is bizarre," he noted cheerfully. "Not to worry. You'll get used to it pretty fast."

"I hope so," Naira replied. "It would be really nice if I find out I have some abilities myself."

"You do," Cara confirmed. "You wouldn't have come all this way if you didn't."

She twisted in her seat, wincing at the pain and gasping, as she tried to shift her position again. "You'd think I'd learn about the painful movements," she quipped. "You really would, but I just keep moving too fast, too suddenly, and paying the price."

"And that's pretty normal for somebody who's been wounded, like you have," Cara noted, not even looking at

Naira.

"Why do I feel like you know an awful lot more about me than I know about me?" Naira asked Cara.

"Because it's quite possibly true," Cara replied. "I see energy threads, and yours are a mess." Her tone was blunt and yet somehow not insulting.

Naira stared at her new friend. "A mess?"

"Yes, and you've started to unravel the mess," Cara noted, "but you're not there yet."

"Do you see the same mess with Scott?"

At that, her lips twitched, and then she nodded. "I do."

"Good," Naira said. "I mean, if I've got things to sort out, it makes me feel better to think he does too."

At that, Cara burst out laughing. "Got it. Misery loves company."

"Well, let's just hope that if it's not misery that we're both in, we are at least both working on cleaning up our acts."

"You guys are working on it," Cara confirmed, "and that's a good thing. Strife in a scenario like this is not good for anybody."

Naira noted that Cara didn't really define what *this* was.

They weren't on the road very long, when all of a sudden, Calum hit the brakes hard, and he started swearing.

"What's the matter?" Naira asked. Cal tried to take the SUV in a hard right, then changed direction. She looked around and realized they had other vehicles chasing them. "Ah, hell. I gather I took too long this morning."

He snorted. "This isn't about you," Cal replied. "Ladies, let the rest of the team know."

Cara replied calmly, "I already have."

"We need to get rid of them," Cal shared. "Otherwise,

we're … I don't want any of us taken captive."

At that, Little Calum shifted sleepily against his mother. Mariana looked at him, trying to keep the worry from her voice and her expression. "It's all right. Go back to sleep, little one."

But the vehicle shifted from side to side, and Naira knew that soon Little Calum would wake up, and a howl would break loose. Who could blame him?

This was now starting to look like they were in deep trouble. Naira had to trust in the team. She had put her lot in with Scott, after spending what seemed like a lifetime waiting for a second chance, so she wasn't about to blow it right now. She waited, tensing up as Cal changed lanes and took hard corners again and again and again.

"We have another vehicle coming up behind us," Cara stated.

"It's Terk." Cal didn't say anything more and just continued to drive.

"There's a weird atmosphere all of a sudden," Naira noted, looking around. "What's happening?"

"Trying to put up a smokescreen," Cara replied.

Naira looked at her funny. "Can I help?"

Cara raised her eyebrows in surprise and then nodded. "Why not," she murmured. "It's your life too." And, on that odd note, Cara gave Naira basic instructions. "Sit back and close your eyes. Don't open them for any reason. Now mentally surround this vehicle with as much smoke as you can dream up in your mind."

"Even if it's not real?"

"Believe me. Your mind will make it real, if you put enough energy into it," she explained. "And, if there's ever a time to learn, it's when you're under pressure like this, right now, because panic helps you to really drive that energy forward."

Naira closed her eyes and, following Cara's simple instructions, tried hard. By the time she opened her eyes, it didn't seem like there was any difference. "I can't do it," she cried out in frustration.

"Well, if you would look again," Calum noted, "you already have. The vehicles aren't around us anymore."

She carefully twisted to look out the back window. "Wow. Where did they go? Did you lose them?"

"It was a combined effort," Cara added, fatigue in her voice.

"It really does take more than one person to do stuff like this. I can't believe that you managed to do it," Naira told Cara, staring at her.

Half a smile later, Cara shared, "You did too. I used your energy to pull in what I needed, and I can't do that very often. I just basically made our energy available to Terk, who's driving behind us."

Some of this was just straight-up crazy talk, too far-fetched for Naira to understand, but she wouldn't say anything now—or maybe ever. At the moment, they were out of danger, and that was worth a lot. She looked at the others, and they seemed to be far calmer than she was. "I gather you guys have had a little bit longer to get used to all this stuff."

"We've had a little bit longer, yes," Lorelei confirmed. "I do trust these men, and I know this team functions at a very high level, especially in times of crisis. I was also attacked and left for dead. There is no doubt that I would be dead, if they hadn't saved me."

At that, Naira winced. "Right, thank you for that. Please

put it down to the fact that this is all new to me."

"You don't have to explain it to us," Mariana said. "This is relatively new to all of us, but what we're finding—as if it was common knowledge—is that we all have some abilities."

"Seriously?" Naira asked.

Mariana nodded. "Not necessarily abilities that we're prepared to work with right now, but, when it comes to life and death, it's amazing just how much that life force and our need to survive gives us abilities to look after each other," she noted. "That's what I've learned through all this. And I know that I don't have special skills anywhere near everybody else's, but, when it comes to keeping a connection with the man I love, believe me. I will do a lot to keep that connection in place."

"I would too if I knew how," Naira muttered. "I didn't even know what he did before this."

"Most of us didn't," Cara agreed. "I'm just the anomaly here."

Naira looked at her and asked, "What is your story, Cara?"

"Terk hired me to keep Rick alive," she stated bluntly. "And, when it came time to detach, I realized just how much of me that I'd lost in the process and how much of him that I had gained—and vice versa, making it not so much him and me but a *we* now."

Naira blinked several times at that bit of an explanation.

Cara gave her a dry smile. "Yeah, go figure. I knew it was a possibility. I just didn't realize it would become such a big issue for me personally," she shared. "I've worked with a lot of nearly dead and dying patients in my life. I just hadn't put any thought into what would happen if I had to go too deep in order to save somebody. The bottom line is that Rick was my test case, and there is now a bond between us that I could never imagine losing in a million years," she murmured. "And I'll do everything I can to keep that now."

It sounded unbelievable to Naira's ears, but Cara was an intensely serious woman, and what she described sounded so incredibly possible that it was hard to even imagine that Cara's words were anything but the truth. Naira knew she had an awful lot more to learn and to understand, but wow. She shook her head. "The fact that what you just said even made sense to me is a bit of an eye-opener too," Naira admitted.

"Ha, wait until you're around here longer," Cara added, with a smile. "There is so much to learn. Terk tried to recruit me quite a while ago, and I wasn't too interested at that time. Now I am, and my abilities will increase a lot the longer I'm around them."

"And you're saying that those of us without abilities might end up with abilities after this?" Naira asked in confusion.

"You've always had abilities if that's the case," Cara stated. "According to Terk, we all have abilities. We just don't use them. And, in Terk's case, he's used them most of his life, finally putting together this amazing team with such extraordinary abilities to assist in the military world."

"I can't imagine that the military world was ready for somebody like Terk," Naira said in astonishment.

At that, Calum smirked and added, "You know what? I don't think anybody is ready for Terk. He's a person aligned to himself."

Naira nodded slowly. "I didn't even think about refusing him when he told me that Scott was down and needed help. I thought, at the time, that it was as much my own need to see him as anything."

"He didn't force you by any means," Calum noted. "That's not something that we can do, not even Terk," he murmured. "So don't think that he influenced your decision at all. However, he would have known how much you care, and that alone would have been something that he needed, just like that connection that Cara was speaking about."

Cara nodded. "Life and death has the ability to make us even more effective and to utilize energy in a way that we consciously didn't realize we could."

"And is it conscious versus subconscious?" Naira asked.

"Most of the time, with Terk, it's always conscious," Cal replied. "But, for a lot of us, getting to that place took a lot of subconscious efforts. And now that most of us on the team are there, we can see how far we've come. We've done a lot of work in this line for a long time," he murmured. "And it's amazing, and it's wonderful, but it's also pretty unnerving. So we understand if not everybody is on board in quite the same way."

"Why? I think I'll be on board," Naira added in fascination. "Even more so if I thought there were any abilities to be developed."

"In that case," Cal said, "welcome aboard because no way Terk would have brought you on without that being a fact."

She stared at him in shock and then looked at Cara, who just nodded.

"The seeds have to be there," Cara noted. "Otherwise it doesn't work for anybody."

Naira sat back, stunned. "Good God," she murmured. "That's not quite what I expected when I came here."

"No?" Calum asked, with a smile. "Yet it looks to be

what you found."

Naira nodded. "And I think I'm okay with that."

SCOTT WAITED, WATCHING his GPS tracker on his phone, as Calum pulled into the underground parking lot and quickly ushered everybody out of the vehicle and into the elevator. Scott opened the penthouse door within minutes. "This is home."

Naira turned, surprised to find Scott here.

He smiled. "Welcome to your home for a time. It's a safe house."

"Wow," Lorelei said. "MI6 by any chance?"

He nodded. "We need their help right now," he stated bluntly.

"If people could only imagine what their taxes sometimes pay for," Cara noted, shaking her head.

"Doesn't matter what it pays for right now," Calum replied. "That money will keep you all safe."

"Got it." Cara nodded.

Everybody wandered the huge space in shock.

"This is stunning," Naira admitted. "I never expected to be in a place quite so high-end."

"Well, it may not happen again," Scott admitted cheerfully. "So enjoy it."

"Are there supplies?" That question came from Mariana. "Little Calum here needs some food and distractions."

"Absolutely," Scott replied. "It's supposed to be fully stocked. Let's go check. It also has four bedrooms, so go pick out a room each," he added. "I was told that one also has a bunk in it for Little Calum."

"Good, I'll take that one," Mariana said. "Chances are he'll want to stay with me anyway."

Cal smiled. "Let's go check out the kitchen." He led them through the penthouse. Soon everybody opened the fridge and the cupboards to see what food was available.

Naira laughed. "Looks like they saw us coming," she said, with a grin. "Quite a lot of food is here."

"A group of us would go through a lot of food pretty fast though," Mariana added, with a note of warning.

Scott smiled and nodded. "I'm sure we can get more when we need it."

"Good," Mariana replied. "This will be fun. Too bad there's no pool."

"There is in the hotel itself, plus in the condo section, but those are out of bounds for us." At that, all the women frowned, turned, and stared at Scott. He nodded. "Nobody is to know you're here, and you're not to have contact with anyone outside of actual team members. If you need something, you contact us, and that includes everything—like ordering pizza," he stated firmly.

"No contact with the outside world. You got it?" he repeated. Then he turned and looked at everyone, waiting for their agreement. When they did, and Scott was satisfied, he turned and looked back at Naira. "So, I get that you're tired, that you're frustrated, and that you don't want things to continue like it are," he said, "but this needs to happen right now."

"I understand," she replied, "and I'm happy to hole up here for a while. I presume the TVs work and all. I see even a small library over there, but I doubt it will hold my attention for long."

"I don't know," Scott replied. "You might be surprised."

"Food first and then we'll see. Are you staying?" she asked.

Scott looked at her, nodded. "Yes, but, before you get too excited, we'll be taking shifts."

"And who'll come next?" she asked.

"Probably Cal because of his family," Scott noted.

Naira totally agreed with that. And realized that Gage and Rick might also rotate in, since Lorelei and Cara were here as well. Naira nodded. "That makes a lot of sense. And I'm sure that Little Calum will be happier, having his dad here, though he's proven to be a little trooper."

"That's the hope," Scott agreed. "We're trying to keep the stress down for everybody. This is a good place to stay. Nobody knows you're here, and, as far as we're concerned, this is where you'll be for a little while."

"Wow," she said, "when you say, *a little while*, I get a bit worried."

Scott shrugged. "Can't be more definitive at this time. We just don't know how long it'll take."

"I know." She nodded. "How are you holding up with all this?"

"I'm frustrated. We're expecting the attack to be imminent, and, as much as I would like to be there as part of the action, I realize I am the weak link at the moment, though nobody is 100 percent yet."

"Of course. You are still healing, the most recent team member to emerge from a coma," Naira stated. "And I can imagine how Brody will feel when he wakes up and finds that all the action has happened without him."

Scott nodded. "Good point. He'll be pissed, just like I was. And we'll laugh, and we'll tease him, and we'll bug him about it, until the end of time," Scott added. "Because all would be just fine in that scenario, since he would be awake and okay. And we'll do anything we can to make that happen."

She grimaced, nodding slowly. "I understand." Naira hesitated, looked around. "So it seems that everybody has a partner. Does Brody have one?"

"None that I know of," Scott replied, "though we didn't know about half of these ladies either, just like they didn't know about you. That would be a better question for Terk. He knows that shit more than any of us."

"Which is also odd," Naira noted, studying Scott closely. "I would have thought you guys would talk about things more."

"No, not at all," he disagreed. "We're busy, always on the job, working or sleeping in shifts, frequently out around the world in small teams or pairs."

"Got it." She turned and looked around. "Well, I'm not sure what we'll do about food, but I'm hungry."

At that, Little Calum piped up. "I'm hungry too." And he looked over at her with a big grin, rubbing his hands together.

She asked Mariana, "Hey, Mom, what can we have?"

Mariana laughed. "Give me just a few minutes to check out the rest of this kitchen," she replied, "and I'll come up with something. How's that?" And she turned toward the kitchen again.

"I can help," Naira offered immediately. "I'm certainly not expecting you to look after me," she murmured. "I was just curious about what this little man will eat."

"Everything," Mariana stated, "but, from the looks of what I've seen of your appetite, you do too."

"Wow." She gasped in amusement. "I'm stunned that

anybody noticed."

"Get over it," Cara quipped, with a smile. "No secrets here."

"Yeah, and usually we tease Tasha about eating enough to rival any man," Lorelei shared, "so guess you're next on the list."

And, with that, everybody started to tease each other, as if they were on holiday. Naira looked over at Scott, watching, as all the women joked and laughed.

THERE WAS A naturalness to this exchange that gave Scott a moment of pause, but he realized they were just trying to make the best of a difficult situation. He had to admire that. Too often it wasn't the case with people, and they weren't too interested in helping to make the best of anything. But these women were special. He knew it; he felt it. They were the partners of all his best friends and brothers-in-arms. A group so close that most people couldn't begin to understand if he tried to explain it.

But he also knew that right here, right now, there was no need to explain. And that made him feel even better. He'd already sent off messages, letting people know that they were in position. Cal had left immediately, hoping he might pick up the tail again somewhere and lead them away from the area. Scott also knew Terk was nearby but not likely to come up here, and Scott couldn't blame him for that. With so much other shit happening, Terk was probably doing some reconnaissance of his own.

When Scott's phone rang a little while later, he stepped away from the chatter going on in the kitchen and answered it. "Hey, Terk. What's up?"

"You've got company."

At that, Scott sucked in his breath. "Already? Do you think we were followed?"

"I'm not sure whether you were followed or if it's just a general reconnaissance visit," Terk replied. "No way to know, but, as long as you're locked in safe, you should be okay."

"What will you do?"

"I'm coming up behind him," Terk noted, his tone relaxed, yet, at the same time, intense.

"We need to get our hands on more people to get more answers," Scott stated. "If this guy has any answers, I want to know what's going on."

"I'm just giving you a heads-up because I saw somebody trying to get into the apartment."

"Well, we shut off the elevator," Scott confirmed.

"Did you check the balcony?"

"I'm doing that right now." As Scott stepped out, a gunman dropped down from the platform above him and smiled.

"Hang up the phone," he ordered, his voice harsh, the gun pointed at Scott. "I see an awful lot of people inside that apartment, and I'll just start popping them if you don't."

Immediately Scott hung up, knowing that Terk had heard the intruder's voice anyway. "It's already hung up." Scott held up his phone.

"Now toss the phone overboard," he stated, "and I mean it. Right down to the streets below."

Not even hesitating for a second, Scott tossed it. He wasn't sure if anybody inside had picked up on what was happening out here, but he hoped so. Nobody here was dense; it's just that they weren't prepared like Scott was. "Interesting that you found me," Scott noted. "What is it that you want?"

"Taking all of you as hostages would be a bit much to deal with," he replied, "so I'll have to make sure to dwindle down the numbers slightly."

Scott's blood ran cold at that. "What's the point of hostages?" he asked. "You can just tell us what you want."

"And why would I do that?" he asked, swinging around the gun for effect.

"You must have some reason for being here," Scott shared, with his own sarcasm. "So I presume you're waiting for somebody else to join you, or you're expecting to check in with someone."

"Why do you say that?" the gunman asked, frowning at him.

"Because you haven't got your own reason for being here," Scott replied impatiently. "So you're obviously not the kingpin of the outfit."

The gunman just glared at Scott, already irritated.

"Right, so what are you? Some kind of catwalk guy who somehow managed to get to the roof?"

"I come up this building all the time," the gunman replied. "Usually I skydive off it."

Scott nodded, noting the intruder's odd outfit. "Ah, and that's how you're planning on escaping, huh?"

"Why not? I mean, I'm up here for business as it is, so I might as well enjoy my escape."

"Got it, but you still haven't told me what you want."

"You're supposed to know already," he stated.

Scott stared at him. "What?"

The guy looked at him, pulled out his phone, and, as

soon as somebody answered on the other side, he spoke. "I'm in position, and I've disarmed the first man on the balcony. I'm not sure who all else is here. You guys can come up now."

There was talk on the other end of the call, and the gunman frowned. "Yeah, I can," he replied, "but you told me that you were coming on up." He listened, glared into the phone, and then put away his cell. "They'll be a bit," he told Scott, "so you might as well get comfortable."

"Great. They'll be a bit, *huh*? That doesn't sound very good—for you."

"It doesn't sound bad either though," the man noted, with a shrug.

"They'll probably wait and see if I have any more friends coming in," Scott shared.

"Either way, we'll make sure that you're the first one to go."

"Sorry to disappoint you but the only one dying today is you," Scott declared. "However, you said *we*, so it's really not all about you wanting something or not. You came here to kill."

"I didn't say that," he replied.

"Well, you arrived with a weapon, prepared to use it," Scott noted. "Most cops or soldiers would say you came prepared to kill. So are you now trying to tell me that that's not what you're planning?"

The gunman glared at him. "Keep it up, and I'll make sure it is."

But, with Terk on his way, maybe already in the building, Scott just had to keep this guy talking. "You still haven't told me what you want," he repeated. "Maybe we can settle this peaceably. Obviously you are a guy who likes his sport."

"Sure, why not?" he asked. "It's the adrenaline rush."

"Ah, and that's why you're doing what you're doing, is that it?"

He shifted slightly.

"Listen. If you're not part of the main team doing this," Scott explained, "you probably should know that they've already killed off every one of the locals they've hired up to this point."

The gunman stared at Scott for a long moment. "You're just trying to make me nervous." He shook his head. "It won't work. I'm made of sterner stuff."

And, of course, nothing Scott could say would shake this guy's belief. "That's fine," Scott noted. "I mean, if you hadn't made me toss my phone over the balcony, I could have showed you pictures of the last few guys they hired. They're dead—as in *dead*, dead."

At that, Cara stepped out from behind Scott, Naira at her side. Cara waved her phone at the gunman. "I've got a few pictures on my phone. You want to see them?" she asked helpfully, as she looked over at the gunman.

He immediately pointed the gun at her and said, "Step away from him."

Immediately she took several steps farther from Scott. "You intruded on our apartment, where just women and children are, plus poor Scott here, who's already injured. So what's your game plan?" she asked curiously. "I mean, you surely have one, right?"

"He phoned his boss," Scott shared, with half a smirk. "I think they're just waiting to see whether he survives for the next few minutes or to decide if it's worth them making the trip."

But Cara was a smart cookie and would have already realized that.

CHAPTER 13

N AIRA STEPPED OUT and faced the gunman. "We were just getting ready for sandwiches and cookies," she said. "Do you want some?"

"No, I don't want any cookies," the gunman snapped. "What's wrong with you people? Can't you see I'm holding a gun?"

She looked at it and nodded. "Yeah, you are. I'm just not too sure what it is you want us to do about it. You can put it down if you want," she noted casually. "I mean, otherwise someone will surely take it from you eventually." He just stared. She smiled. "And, yes, I'm probably crazy," she noted. "I spent way too much time as a kid playing stupid games."

"What are you talking about?" the gunman roared. "Never mind, just stop talking."

Obediently Naira closed her mouth and just stared at him.

However, he couldn't stand it. "What the hell was that all about anyway?"

But she kept her mouth closed—as if she were now incapable of answering. He stared at her, getting more uneasy by the minute.

Cara snickered.

The intruder glanced at her and asked, "Is she like, you

know?" Then he made a circular motion alongside his head.

"You mean, is she stupid or not quite all there?" Scott asked helpfully.

"Yeah, look at her," the gunman said.

"I know. She's special," Scott replied, with a smirk.

"Yeah, psycho," the intruder muttered. "Jesus, I wasn't expecting to find a bunch of fruit loops here."

"Well," Scott added, "we're just here having a holiday. I'm still not sure what you're here for." Then he looked closer at the gun. "Wow, I guess that part's obvious, but I don't understand why."

"What do you mean, you don't understand why?" he asked, staring. "You were supposed to be expecting us."

"I'm supposed to expect you?" He frowned, shrugged, and shook his head. "Wow, I don't think too many people expect to have guns pulled on them when they're making lunch."

The other guy just glared at him, and then his phone rang. He held the gun up higher as he answered his phone. "What the hell's going on?" he asked. "And why aren't you here? … No, I know. … No, you're not. … Well, sure they're talking. They're talking lots, but nothing they're saying makes any sense," he said in frustration. "What the hell do you want me to do with these guys?" He paused, listening. "Yeah, yeah, sure, I guess." But he frowned, then he stared at the phone.

Then he spoke again. "How come you're not coming? That was the deal. I would come up here. You guys would take over, then I would jump away and get out of this," he stated. "That was the deal, and you're not following through. I don't like that," he stated in a cranky mood.

Naira didn't think he would like what was about to

come either. At least if all she'd heard from the team was true.

"Yeah, yeah, yeah. I know, that's fine," the gunman snapped, "but just hurry it up. This isn't my scene." He shook his head. "I know. I'm the one who had the access, and, yeah, I left you ropes and everything. So use that to come over from the other penthouse." And, with that, he hung up and then smiled at the others.

"Now you're in trouble," the intruder stated, but something was almost comical about his delivery, as if to say he'd been waiting this whole time for confirmation that shit really would happen, and now it would finally come down on these people in the apartment—while the intruder remained outnumbered and uncomfortable, even with a gun. It made for an unfortunate scenario.

Scott and Cara shared a knowing look.

Naira wished she understood what message had just passed between them.

Scott smiled and told Cara, "I don't think he really understands, does he?"

"Hell no he doesn't," Cara noted sadly. "It's kind of sad really because he's so young to die."

"Just like all the other ones," Scott reminded her.

"And that's just wrong too," Cara added in frustration. Just enough truth was in her tone that the gunman turned toward her.

"Are you guys seriously on that again?"

"We don't have to be," Cara murmured. "I get it. You don't believe us, so whatever. I just think it's sad."

"What's sad?" he asked, rolling his eyes. "That I'll die so young?"

"Yes," she confirmed, "and it's even sadder that you

don't believe us, and we'll have to watch as a sniper takes you out. You've got some guy out there who set you up to do his dirty work. Now you've gone down the pathway for a kidnapping or armed robbery here, and you don't even realize what he's done."

"He hasn't done anything," the gunman argued. "I volunteered."

At that, Naira looked at him. "Why?"

"Because of the money. He was just looking for somebody to get him into this penthouse. He told me that it was his and that you guys are part of the group that cheated him out of it. And now you'll pay for it."

"Well, we didn't cheat him out of anything," Scott declared. "And the fact that you don't know that this penthouse belongs to MI6 is absolutely flabbergasting." Scott stared at him.

The gunman looked at him in shock. "What are you talking about? MI6 doesn't own penthouses like these. They're just rundown government workers."

"They're also secret agents," Scott added, with an equally surprised look at the man. "So, of course, they need safe houses. You don't want a safe house where everybody will expect you to be, do you?"

The intruder frowned, then shrugged. "Whatever. It kind of makes more sense if it is MI6 in a way because this guy's been cheated. So I don't really care what the story is. I just want to get my money and to get out."

"You really expect this guy who's lying to you to bring your money here?" Scott asked in astonishment.

"Sure, and I'll take it back out the way I came in," he replied. "Well, actually I'll just go straight down with it, but that's nothing to you."

When another ten minutes went by, as they all remained silent on the balcony, Naira asked, "So where's your buddy?"

"I don't know," the gunman snapped.

"Like I said, we're just here, out in the sun, enjoying being here," Scott noted in a conversational tone, surprising even Naira. "This is our holiday."

"That's just bullshit. How can you have a holiday at an MI6 penthouse?" the intruder asked. "Isn't that right there proof that you're lying?"

"My father works for them," Naira lied convincingly. The gunman stared at her in shock. She shrugged. "Guess who won't be impressed that you pulled a gun on us?"

"I don't give a shit," the gunman snapped, obviously getting more nervous. He looked around. "Where is Daddy anyway?"

"Back in the office," Naira replied, with a smile. "Where would you expect him to be? Do you think they aren't allowed to personally use certain buildings that they have all around the world? Of course they are," she declared, with a slight mocking tone to her voice.

He immediately took umbrage at that. "Don't talk to me like that, bitch," he snapped.

She laughed, shrugged off the insult. "I expected a citizen *like you* to know something."

"How do you know I'm a citizen?" he asked nervously.

She stared at him. "Seriously?"

He just glared.

"Well, for one, you have the accent, and, for another"— she studied him intently—"who else but a local would understand that they could jump off this building? It's hardly a tourist attraction."

He continued to glare at her. "So what if I've been

around a bit?" he stated. "That's got nothing to do with it."

"Yeah, well," she disagreed, with a knowing head tilt. "At least we can get your name from your gravestone," she added, with a smile.

"That's enough of that too," he snapped. "You guys are just full of shit."

"Yep," she agreed, her smile growing bigger. "Apparently you don't understand what that means for you. Too bad."

"It means *nothing*," he argued, still glaring at her. "I haven't done anything wrong."

At that, she stopped and stared. "Are you seriously saying that? You're the one who's standing here, waving a gun at us."

He looked down at the gun, as if surprised that he still had it in his hands. "I'm just trying to make a few bucks," he replied. "It's got nothing to do with me that he's after you."

"Oh, Lord." Naira shared a look with Scott in fascination, pointing at their intruder. "He's really not that stupid, is he?"

"I think so," Scott agreed. "I was really hoping he wasn't, but he's just so innocent to the world, yet nothing we can do about it."

"I hear you," Naira agreed.

Cara had been mostly silent until now and turned toward their intruder. "You know what? If you don't mind, I'll go on inside," she said. "Plus there's fresh coffee by now, and I could use a cup." And not even giving him a chance to say anything, she turned and walked back inside.

SCOTT NO LONGER thought that there would be no way out

of this, even as he considered the sounds of the two men approaching getting closer and closer—most likely Terk and Cal … or more gunmen.

Then Naira stepped on the balcony closer to Scott and shielded her eyes from the sun. She gasped. "Oh my God." Her tone switched from surprise to awareness. "You're the one from the hospital. I couldn't see for the sun before," she explained.

He looked at her and frowned. "No, I'm not."

But something in his voice confirmed her words to be true. "You work at the hospital with her."

And then Scott realized that this was the guy he'd seen down at the end of the hallway. "So, you're a bigger part of this after all," he noted.

The intruder shook his head. "No, I was just supposed to pick her up at the hospital. That's all."

"Interesting, when she ended up dead in a dumpster," Naira added, as just then two more men arrived, coming down from the small overhang above them. She stared from one to the other. "And you guys were from the hospital too," she stated, shaking her head. "Wow, what is this, old home week?"

"Not for you," one of them said, raising his gun.

She cried out when Scott rushed forward, shoving her behind him.

The gunman laughed. "Oh, isn't that cute," he quipped. "You really think you'll save her this time?"

"Well, so far you haven't done a very good job of taking her out," Scott murmured. "So I figured stupidity still had to be coming into play."

The second gunman to speak just glared at him and raised the gun in Scott's direction. "That's hardly fair," he replied. "And I'm not the idiot this guy is." And, with that, he turned, looked over at the first intruder, and said, "Thanks. You can go now."

The guy looked at him with relief. "Well, thank God for that."

"Here. You want this?" He held up a small bag.

"Yeah, I do," he replied, looking hopeful. "I'm so out of here."

The man raised his handgun and fired a single shot in the center of the first gunman's forehead. In shocked astonishment, he slowly sank to the floor of the balcony.

"See? He didn't even see that coming," the second gunman said, turning to address his silent buddy. "I told you. They're all just idiots."

"What they're not is trained military," Scott murmured, as he stared at the two remaining gunmen. "And they don't kill people quite as easily as you do."

"You got that straight." He sneered at Scott.

"You guys have put us through a ton of shit, and we don't appreciate it," Scott shared.

The head gunman raised an eyebrow and glared at him.

Scott nodded. "All we were trying to do is go from one day to the next."

"Well, that isn't happening anymore," the lead gunman announced. "People are pissed at us because we supposedly screwed up, and we'll blame you for that."

"You're blaming me because you screwed up?" It was easy to follow their words, but the logic was definitely leaving a lot to be desired.

"Just fuck off," the lead guy said, as he raised his gun again.

"Remember," his buddy added. "We've got to make sure

they're all dead."

"Oh, we can start with this one," the head gunman stated. "That way the others would line up quite nicely. We can just pop them all."

"You can't," Naira cried out.

"Why not?" he asked, looking at her with a glare. And then he smiled. "You know what? You're right. I should take you out first. That'll just piss him off, but it would make me happy," he stated, with a brighter smile. "You've been nothing but trouble since this whole thing started."

"I didn't do anything but come over here because a friend of mine was hurt," she argued. "I don't even know who you guys are or why you're doing this."

He looked at her. "Seriously?"

She nodded. "Yes, seriously."

"Wow, then you're even more in the dark than I thought," he replied. "This guy was in the dark"—he pointed to his dead patsy—"but apparently you were even worse."

She glared at him. "And I get that's somehow funny for you, but the least you can do is explain it."

With that, he mocked her in a singsong voice. "*The least you can do is explain it.*" Then his tone turned serious. "Like hell. There's a contract on you and as many of this guy's team as possible," he stated. "If we hadn't caught you being picked up at the airport, no way in hell we could have tracked you down."

"Still, why were you even at the airport? And why would you know I was there?" Naira asked, staring at him in surprise. "It's not as if you knew I was coming."

"Well, we wondered, and we did pick up a message," the lead guy confirmed. "But it was kind of by accident that we found Terk close to the airport. Normally we can't see him at all, and that's pretty pissy too. But, once we caught his track at the airport, we just followed him. And, for once, we got a lucky break." His smirk turned into a grimace. "Then you turned out to be a complete pain in the ass. So, as far as I'm concerned, you owe us big-time."

"I don't owe you jack shit," she snapped, glaring at him. "And I mean that with the best of intentions."

He snorted. "Everybody's always so fucking cheeky," he noted. "I'm not used to that with somebody who is facing down a gun."

"You're trying to shoot me," she said. "What is it you expect me to do? Sit here and whimper, pleading for my life?"

"Yeah, honestly I do. I do want to hear that. I especially want to hear you plead for this guy's life," he added, as he raised the gun in Scott's direction.

"Oh, I might do it for him," she admitted, "but don't you want to tell me what this is all about first?"

"A contract," he said, rolling his eyes. "Are you too stupid not to understand what that means?"

"So, somebody's paying you to kill me?"

He nodded. "And it's because you're connected to this guy. I mean, if you weren't, if you'd have ditched him a long time ago, you'd be safe right now. You would be back at home—or whatever nasty little hollow you call home—and you wouldn't have anything to do with this," he explained, wearing a big smile. "It's just your dumb luck that you hooked up with a guy who's pissing everybody off. And guess what?" he said. "There's a contract on his head and all the rest of his team."

"But the team is dead," she stated, her gaze going from

Scott to the gunman and back.

He looked at Scott and laughed. "You kept her in the dark, did you? What a joke," he sneered. "No way in hell that you'll keep lies like that afloat. You do know that relationships are supposed to be built on so much more."

"Yeah," Scott agreed. "The problem is, when you guys are out there shooting away at us, it'll scare her off."

That seemed to send this gunman off in a fit of gleeful laughter. "Oh my God, you are so right there." And then he got an ugly look on his face. "But you're still just pissing me off. We should have had this job done weeks ago."

"And were you told to kill this guy?" she asked, staring at the body and then hurriedly pulling away her gaze.

"Yep, just part of it," he replied. "No threads left behind."

"Oh, and what about you?" Naira asked him. "I mean, you're just doing a contract, so aren't you a thread then too?"

He glared at her. "Don't even fucking start with me," he yelled. "We finish this job, and we're good to go. Millions of dollars will hit our bank account, and we're out of here."

She stared at him, and her jaw dropped.

Scott had never seen her act before, and he was quite impressed. She had this down pat.

"So wait," Naira began, "hang on a minute. Did you take this contract without money upfront?"

"Jesus, of course not. What kind of an idiot do you think I am? We got a deposit of course," he said. "I think I fucking know how to do my job."

"Well, I run my own business too," she stated. "Nothing like yours," she added, even managed to get a humbleness into her voice. "I mean, I'm just a, you know, a little graphic artist."

The other man snickered.

"But still, I just can't help but wonder what's to stop them from killing you, once you've done the job," she noted, "unless you've got some kind of insurance of course."

"Of course we do," the lead gunman replied. "We're not idiots."

"No, of course not," she murmured, once again giving him a nod and stroking his ego. "One more thing. Did anybody say anything about why they are even doing this? I just don't get it."

"Doesn't matter. Something about these guys pissed off a lot of people before the contract went out," he explained. "And our job is not to ask why."

"No, of course not," she agreed. "You won't get a second contract if you sit there and ask too many questions, would you?"

He shook his head. "No, you sure as hell don't, and we plan on doing this for quite a while."

"So, you didn't charge enough money for these contracts to retire?" she asked. "I mean, I don't know how many guys were on his team"—she pointed at Scott—"but isn't that putting yourself at a lot of risk?"

"Don't worry. We're being well paid for it," he said. "Chances are quite good that, if we're smart, we won't have to do another job ever," he declared. "But that means that you guys all get to die."

"Why us?" she asked, staring at him. "I mean, seriously why us women? It's these guys you want."

"Yep, but like I said, as long as you are part of it, you are getting taken out too."

She frowned.

"Don't worry about it," he told her. "I'll make it fast for

you."

"Thanks," she said. "I appreciate that. Also a little boy is in there. Could you make sure he doesn't suffer too?"

He stared at her. "There's a kid?"

She nodded. "Yeah."

"Nobody said anything about kids. This is the first I've heard of it."

"It's a little boy." Naira smiled. "He's really adorable."

The head guy looked over uneasily at his buddy.

"You did get extra money for him, didn't you?" she asked innocently.

"They're collateral damage," his silent partner spoke up, "and no way I'll get extra money."

"Shit, man," the lead guy added, "I've got two boys of my own."

"I know. I know. I do too. Remember?"

And then the head gunman shook his head. "Absolutely no option here, especially now that they're all here together." He turned and glared at Scott. "You know this shit is your fault, right?"

Scott stared at him. "What's my fault?"

"If you hadn't brought them all here together," the gunman explained, "we wouldn't have had to kill that kid."

"You don't have to kill him now," Scott stated. "That's all on you if you do."

The gunman shook his head. "No, you don't get it. No going back on this. We're committed." As he raised the gun, he added, "Look. The faster we do this, the better." And just as he went to fire, Scott tossed himself sideways, knocking Naira to the ground. She cried out in pain as she hit the concrete. Scott heard the bullet whiz past him, but then came a weird *ping*.

Scott smiled as the lead gunman dropped down, now lifeless.

Scott immediately snagged the loose handgun and bounded to his feet, holding it on the second gunman.

The guy looked at his buddy on the ground, then up at Scott, and asked, "What the hell did you do?"

"I didn't do anything," Scott confirmed. "And I'm sorry, but, in this case, the people who hired you, those guys clean up. They don't pay anybody. All they do is make you do the dirty work, and then they kill you."

"Yeah, but they took him out first."

"That was probably not intentional because he fired at me and missed. They would have set that up, assuming he was at least doing his job, and then leave you here to face me," Scott noted in a calm tone.

"No, no, no, no, this can't be happening," the last gunman wailed. "We're getting the hell out of Dodge. This is the end. We won't do this no more."

"Well, you're right about this being the end," Scott agreed. "And honestly, if I were you, I'd get the hell out of the open like that because they'll come back around to get you with the next shot."

"Get who?" the guy asked.

"You," Naira replied, as she slowly got to her feet. "A drone took him out."

He looked at her, his face paling. "They have drones?" he asked nervously.

"Yeah," Scott confirmed. "We've seen them take out all kinds of people with those drones." The trouble was, he wasn't sure who the hell was running that drone out there. He could only hope that maybe it was one of Scott's own people. But he couldn't be sure. Scott stared at this last intruder and asked, "What the hell will you do now?"

"I have to finish the job," he said, but panic filled his voice. "I have to. I mean, if they see me finishing it, then I'll be okay."

"If you say so." Scott motioned at the gun in his own hand. "Do you really expect me to just let you stand there and kill me and her?"

The guy looked at him. "I have to," he repeated. "I mean, otherwise I'm dead."

"You're right. Either way, you'll be dead," Naira stated, walking closer to him. "Don't you have a backup plan, like an escape plan?"

He stared at her, as if trying to figure out what she was talking about. "I should, shouldn't I?" he said.

"Yes, you should," she murmured. "I'm surprised you don't."

"He said we didn't need one." He looked down at his friend. "And that, after we took out the other guy, we would be okay."

"And now two of you are gone," Scott noted. "Do you know anything about the guys who hired you?"

He shook his head. "No, not at all. I'm not even part of this business," he muttered. "I was just trying to get the hell out of town and to create a new life somewhere, but I needed money." He desperately looked over at the two of them, as if seeking reassurance that he had made the right decision.

Scott almost felt sorry for him. "When you start killing people like this," he said, "there are always repercussions."

"Yeah, yeah, I know," he replied, "but he said it was safe."

"Safe?" Naira asked in shock. "Safe to *kill* people? Seriously?"

He flushed. "Hey, look. He's a good friend of mine, and I believed him."

"He *was* a good friend of yours," she reminded him gently. "And now he's dead, and the people who hired you took him out. So, if you help us," she offered, "we can try to keep you safe."

He looked at her. "All I've got is an email and a phone number," he noted, "and they put the money in our bank account."

"But did they?" she asked. "If you do banking online, maybe you should check that."

He wanted to, and it was obvious that he really wanted to.

Scott slowly lowered his gun. "Go ahead and check."

The remaining gunman looked at him nervously, pulled out his phone awkwardly, and with lots of glances in their direction, he brought up his bank. "Where's the money?" he whispered, bewildered.

"Either they didn't put it in or they reversed the charges right away," Scott explained. "It's an old trick. It starts to show up, saying this transaction is pending, and then, when you think it's all good, it gets pulled away from you," he murmured. "You think the money is there, and all you have to do is finish the job, and you'll be good to go, but instead you've just been taken for a ride and possibly committed murder too," Scott murmured.

The guy looked like he was ready to cry.

"How many guys did you kill?" she asked him. "Maybe the cops will go easy on you."

He looked at her and slowly shook his head. "No, you don't understand. There won't be cops."

"Why not?" she asked.

"They'll make sure of it. They'll make sure that I don't go anywhere." He looked around, beginning to panic.

"The least you can do is tell us more about them, so we can get them for double-crossing you."

He looked at her, mildly interested for a moment, and then added, "All it'll do is get you killed."

"That is quite possible," she admitted. "After being attacked twice, I understand I will quite possibly spend the rest of my life looking over my shoulder."

"That's exactly how it will be," he told her. "You have to stop them."

"I'd love to, if you want to tell us how."

"I don't know," he wailed, "but they're setting up a plan to take out the main base and to kill off the one guy who's left. He's in some kind of a coma. They thought he wouldn't come back out of it, but now they can't take any chances."

Her heart sank as she glanced at Scott to see a hard glint in his eyes. "Any idea when the attacks are happening?"

"Tomorrow, I think," he said, "but these two dead guys might have changed things. ... God, I'm such an idiot." There was absolutely no misunderstanding what he meant. "It wasn't supposed to be like this," he muttered.

"It never is," Scott agreed, "and killing isn't supposed to be easy either."

The guy looked at him, then slowly nodded. "No, you're right. It isn't. Unfortunately it was just a little too easy." He sighed. "I don't know what that says about me. Except I was desperate."

Naira asked in a soothing tone, "Is there anything else you can tell us? Any names?"

"Yeah, some funny, like, Iranian-sounding name."

"The contract is from another country?"

He nodded. "My buddy said that, on some of the communications, it was almost hard to understand the English. But the higher-ups were pretty adamant about what they wanted."

"Of course they were," Scott said. "Do you have a location?" He named the spot, and that made Scott's eyebrows go up.

"And how do you know that was part of it?"

"Because Dean here," he said, motioning to his dead friend on the ground, "he managed to get a little bit more information out of them. No way he would get into something like this and not have what he needed to make sure that he could get out."

"What do you think now?" she asked him. "Do you think he got enough?"

"No," he murmured.

"They double-crossed him completely," Scott stated.

The remaining gunman nodded. "You guys need to get these assholes, and you need to get them now." He retrieved his phone from his pocket and tossed it to her. "Use whatever you need to, but make sure you get them." He started to back out of the balcony.

"Whoa, whoa, whoa," Scott said, stepping forward. "Where are you going?"

"There's no life for me now," he admitted. "I can't handle jail, not after this," he murmured. "And I can't handle my parents hearing what I've done."

"You sure you don't want to try and explain to them from your perspective?" Naira asked.

He looked at her, tears forming in his eyes. "No," he said. "Sometimes you just go too far down a path that there is no recovery. And, for my mother, this would be a no-recovery point."

"She loves you," Naira reminded him quietly.

"No, she *loved* me."

"Love is not conditional," Naira argued. "We may not love what our loved ones do, but that doesn't stop us from still loving them."

He stared at her and gave her half a smile. "Yeah, you're a romantic," he noted. "I had two girlfriends just the same, and both of them have got sons of mine. Yet I couldn't settle down to marry either one of them."

"And that's too bad," she replied. "I think you've missed out on an awful lot of love in your life."

He stared at her in shock. "And I think," he snapped, "that you spend an awful lot of time looking at life from the sunshine-and-roses perspective. No good ending can come from this."

Scott personally agreed with him, but he wouldn't do anything to make this get ugly. At least not any more uglier than it already was. "So, is there a message you want me to take to them?"

He stared at him. "Would you?"

"I would," Scott promised.

"Yes, of course we would," Naira agreed. "I still think that you need to help us, but, if you're intent on trying to kill yourself, we can't do a whole lot about it."

He looked at her and laughed. "No, sure as hell not," he agreed, then raised his gun to his head.

Almost immediately Scott raised his.

"See? Already you're thinking you should just shoot my gun hand and stop me from getting out of this," he explained, "because you're only looking after yourselves right now. But me? I've got to look after myself."

"And what about your friend?" Scott asked, motioning at the dead man on the ground.

"Yeah, I've got to think about him too and what he would have wanted."

"I gather you were good buddies."

"We were," he noted. "And sometimes buddies like him are all that's left in the world. Everybody else ends up being somebody you don't recognize."

"Just like you maybe?" Scott asked.

"Maybe," he admitted, as he looked over at Scott. "It still doesn't change anything though. I'm not going to jail." And before they had a chance to do anything, he jumped over the edge of the balcony railing.

His gun dropped harmlessly to the ground on the balcony beside them. There was almost no sound of him hitting the ground several floors below.

Naira froze in place, then turned and looked at Scott. "You look," she said. "I can't do it."

At that, he walked over to the edge and looked down. Sure enough, the gunman was on the ground, clearly dead. A crowd was slowly gathering.

Scott pulled out his phone and called Terk.

"I saw," Terk answered. "God damn it."

"Well, we got as much information off him as we could, but, when you guys shot the other guy, he kind of lost it."

When he heard a gasp beside him, he turned to see Naira, staring at him in shock.

Scott just smiled at her. "Terk, if you're okay, I'll call you back in a little bit." As soon as he hung up, he walked over to Naira and said, "Our drone took out Dean."

She stared at him. "How can you be sure?" she cried out. "You said *these guys* were using drones."

"They were, and you're right. That's exactly what they were doing," he noted. "But this drone was operated by one of our own guys."

"How do you know?"

"Because I saw the energy," he stated, with a gentle smile. "And I also got a telepathic message from Terk, letting me know what was going on."

Outrage grew on her face, as she realized she had been sidelined. She tapped him on the shoulder, while a hard finger jabbed his chest. "That's enough of that shit. I want to learn to do what you do. I want to make sure that the next time there's an inside line that I'm in on it too," she growled at him.

He smiled. "I don't have a problem with that. However, it'll take training, and it'll involve a lot of frustration."

"*You* are a lot of frustration," she snapped. But then she threw her arms around his neck and whispered, "I was so scared."

"Well, you sure didn't show it," he said, holding her close. "And believe me. The fact that you didn't fall apart on a deal like that is huge."

"Can we go home now?"

"I'm not sure," he noted. "We'll talk with Terk and see what else has been going on. He should be here in a minute."

"The gunman said that they were preparing for an attack on the main compound."

He nodded, his tone grim. "I heard him." Then he turned; all the other women stood in the living room, on the opposite side of the balcony's double glass doors, obviously aware of what had just happened. He looked over at Little Calum, who appeared to be completely oblivious. Scott raised an eyebrow in Mariana's direction, but she shook her head.

"We were busy in the kitchen," she explained, then whispered something to Lorelei and left the room with Little Calum in her arms.

"Good," Scott murmured. Turning to the others, he said, "I'm not sure what to say, except that the shit is hitting the fan."

"And that's a good thing," Lorelei stated. "I gather bringing us out did the job."

He winced. "We knew it was either an option or a problem," Scott admitted.

"It was more than that," Lorelei added. "It was bait. We were bait."

"It wasn't deliberate bait," Scott corrected. "We were taking you all out to keep you safe. What we didn't expect was to have somebody here within seconds of your arrival."

"With the attack coming tomorrow, we should return to the compound," Lorelei said.

Scott shook his head. "No, they are in the best position to handle this."

"What about Brody?" Naira asked.

"I think that's where Terk wants to go himself," Scott replied. When Naira wanted to protest, he stopped her with a look. "Remember. This is what we do."

She stomped her foot in frustration. "Maybe so," she argued relentlessly. "But Brody's part of the team, and we have to help him."

He smiled at her. "Well, I'm sure Brody would really appreciate that. However, we also have to expect that there is more to this plan than just taking out these gunmen today."

"I hope so," she said, staring at him, "because that was kind of shitty."

He laughed, held her close, turned, and looked back at Lorelei. "The cops will be here soon and will stay for a while," he noted. "So we need to keep that in mind, and we better tell Mariana."

"Nope," she said. "They already headed to their room to watch movies. Little Calum was looking pretty sleepy, so I'm guessing he'll be out before long."

"Can we just take some food into the other room and hope the police can just deal with it?" Naira asked Scott.

"Well, that's the plan. I just don't know how long it will take." But, as it was, it didn't take very long at all.

With the others busy in the dining room, MI6 came and left, removing both bodies from the rooftop balcony in record time, already covering up and moving the body at ground level.

Moments later, they were gone, and Merk stood in the living room, glaring at Scott.

Scott raised both hands in mock surrender. "What do you want me to say?" he asked. "We're all alive. We're all safe."

"Sure," Merk muttered, "but what the hell was that all about with her?"

Naira stepped out of the dining room area into the living room, where the two men remained. Merk just glared at her, but she glared right back. "I get it," she replied, "but, at the same time, what was I supposed to do? Let this guy throw his life away?"

"You were taking chances, and you could have been shot."

"For the record, I have already been shot. In the lung. Then drugged and hit over the head. So, yes," she replied. "I could have been shot *again*, since I was their target not so long ago. And, yes, we were taking chances, but we might have also saved a life. Plus we got info and the kid's phone."

Merk stared at her for a long moment, then turned to look at Scott. "Oh boy."

"Yeah, I know." Scott smiled. "She's a spitfire. Glad she's on our team."

"The team has apparently grown a conscience." Merk looked at her and back at Scott, then started to laugh. "Damn good thing you already had a healthy conscience. In your case, you were being pretty damn stubborn."

"I think that's also the main problem with this guy." She pointed to Scott. "He's the one with the problem."

Scott just looked at her and said, "Seriously?"

"Why not?" She grinned. "I could get a lot of mileage out of this, you know?"

He pulled her close and replied, "No mileage. We'll park this right now."

"Sure," she agreed, but she looked over at Merk. "I did good, didn't I?"

He burst out laughing. "Well, let's just say," he murmured, "that you didn't do half bad."

"There you go," she said, "faint credit, but I'll take it."

He shook his head. "You shouldn't have been involved at all."

"Yeah, well, you know," Scott added, "all these women have something to say about *that*."

"And I wouldn't even have known what was happening on our balcony," Naira explained, "but then Cara told me that I was needed outside."

Scott groaned and shook his head. "Why the hell would she say that?" he cried out. "You were the last person needed out there. We were trying to keep you away from the three gunmen, since you were their most recent primary target. They came here after you."

"And I figured they came after all of us," she argued. "So what the hell? I mean, if they got me, then what difference does it make? Besides, he obviously wasn't too sure what to do with himself, especially after *somebody*"—she turned to glare at Merk—"took out his partner."

Merk just stared at her blandly.

She nodded. "Like I said, somebody took out his partner, left him feeling like he didn't know what to do. I just suggested a few options for him."

Scott laughed.

"I'll go do some reconnaissance with Terk," Merk said, shaking his head. "Do you guys think you can stay out of trouble for once?"

"We'll be happy to stay here and to recuperate," Naira replied, with a bright smile. "You are leaving Scott with us, right?'

"At least for the moment." Then Merk turned and looked at the two of them. "So, while you're enjoying your little *holiday* here, while the rest of us work, do your best to heal." With that, Merk was gone.

She threw her arms around Scott and asked, "What do you think? Can we heal now?"

"On so many levels," he murmured, holding her close.

"Oh." She tilted her head. "Is that what he meant?"

"It's partly what he meant," Scott confirmed, staring at the doorway behind them. "And that was not necessarily a comment I would have expected from Terk's brother."

"Well, if Terk has all those abilities," she noted, "how is it possible that his brother doesn't? I suspect he's just not been willing to develop them or to publicize what he has."

"You could be right," Scott agreed, looking down at her, with a smile. He pulled her close and kissed her lightly.

When he finally lifted his head, she muttered, "We could leave the others to watch their movies on their own."

"Oh? And what did you have in mind?" he asked, one eyebrow raised.

"I was thinking of taking a little private time to heal," she replied, mischief in her eyes. "But we have to be quiet, since Little Calum is nearby."

He looked around and whispered, "Well, it's dark now. It's late, and I'm sure you need a nap."

"You know what? I'm sure I do too," she agreed with a laugh, and he bent down and scooped her up.

"I think that's a hell of a good idea," he stated, then he walked them into their bedroom. He set her on her feet, before turning and locking the door. By the time he turned around, she had already stripped down to her underwear. He let out a big wolf whistle.

She grinned. "You've forgotten," she said, chuckling.

"No way," he declared, holding her still for a moment. "That's not something I could ever forget," he murmured. "You're too damn special for that."

She smiled and added, "Maybe we need something better to remember this all by."

He pulled her close, leading them to the bed, and then proceeded to remind both of them why they'd been compelled to wait these past years for each other to return.

Raising himself up on his elbows, their bodies' slick with sweat from their renewed foreplay, she twisted beneath him with need. He whispered, "You know I never stopped loving you, right?"

She pulled him down to her and whispered, "You know

I never stopped loving you either, right?"

And, with that, he slowly slipped home. She twisted and arched beneath him, her body already primed with need. And he slowly increased his motions, until she softly cried out in his arms. When she came apart, he realized he was the luckiest man in the world. As she dug her nails into his buttocks, he let out a growl and proceeded to pick up the pace, until he was drowning in his own joy.

Collapsing beside her, he whispered, "I might have been a little noisy."

"Yeah," she agreed, "you might have been. However, I'm pretty damn sure Mariana just turned up the TV, so they couldn't hear anything."

He grinned. "I do like being around smart women," he noted contentedly.

"And so you should," she replied, "as long as you include me in that group."

"Of course." He smiled. "You're the smartest of them all."

She burst out laughing. "Let's not push it," she said. "From what I've seen, some pretty impressive women are gathered here."

He grinned. "There are, indeed. You should have fun getting to know each and every one of them. And, by the way," he added, "thank you for coming back to me."

She slid her arms around his neck and whispered, "You're welcome. Thanks for being here, waiting for me."

He pulled her closer, and they went to sleep. Together.

---

*B*RODY?

He shuddered.

Brody came the insistent voice, yet again.

He tried to block it out. It had been yelling and screaming at him for what seemed like forever. He'd done everything he could to make it go away, but still it was persistent. He tried once again to shut it down, but it came back once more.

No, not this time came the calm voice. *We need you. Get up, get out, come back.*

Brody thought it was Terk's voice. He wasn't sure, but maybe? It was hard to tell what Terk's problem was.

But, if Terk called, it meant that he needed something. And, if Terk needed something, Brody would be there for him. Except how could he be sure it was Terk?

It didn't really sound like him; it seemed a long distance away. And then he heard that woman's voice again. "Who the hell was that?" Again came the softer voice.

Come on, Brody. Wake up. Come on. It's time to wake up. You've had a nice nap, but that time is over.

He sighed and twisted. He wanted to sleep some more. He wanted to tell them that he was still too tired and that he still needed sleep, but he didn't think they would care. He tried to block them out yet again, but the male voice returned, insistent and hard.

No, that's enough now. Come out now, on your own, or come out with our help.

Brody slowly opened his eyes, only to see nothing. It was just black out there. He snapped his eyelids closed again. "See? I tried," he muttered.

The female laughed. *Oh no you don't. You don't get off so easy,* she murmured. *Try it again.*

"No."

Yes.

"No."

Yes. And I'm glad to see you've got enough strength to argue, Terk said telepathically.

Brody froze. "Terk?"

Yeah, bud. We'd sure like to see you come back out of where you've been hiding.

"Hiding?" he snapped. Struggling higher and higher through the fog, he fought. How dare Terk say Brody was hiding? He'd never hidden in his life. He always took every fight head-on. There was no hiding in his life. Ever.

When he slowly drifted higher and higher, he looked around. "Where am I?" he cried out, feeling the first visages of fear. "It's dark."

And this time, the woman's voice, with something almost recognizable about it, soothed him. *We're here,* she stated. *We're waiting for you.*

He felt relief at hearing her voice again, but it was couched in a near panic because he didn't know who she was or where she was. "Where am I?" he asked, his voice almost strangled.

You've been in a coma, she stated calmly. *And we need you to come back now.*

"And if I don't want to?" he asked almost bitterly.

Too bad, she murmured. *You need to. Unless, of course, you'll continue to hide.*

He twisted, surging higher and higher again. "I don't hide," he growled, a darkness in his soul overriding everything that they were doing. "I don't know who you are or why you would say that to me," he snapped, "but I don't hide."

Then suddenly it looked like he was … here. He opened his eyes and saw a room. Relief washed through him. It wasn't just darkness. It wasn't a never-ending unwavering blackness surrounding him. As he fully opened his eyes, he looked around. He was in a room, a small bedroom. And he was alone. "Where am I?" he whispered.

You're safe, a woman said quietly. *And I need you to stay safe. All your friends are about to be attacked, and so are you.*

He struggled to toss off all the cloudiness and a bit of fog in his brain. "I don't understand," he muttered. "Where are you?"

I'm here, she stated calmly. *You can talk to me anytime.*

Just then a woman walked into his room. She stopped, looked at him, and smiled. "There you are," she greeted him.

He frowned. *The voice is different*. "You sound surprised."

"Sure," she replied. "I wasn't expecting to see you awake."

He looked at her hard. "Who were you expecting to see?"

She shrugged. "Good question, but not you. I thought you were a goner."

"Well, I'm not," Brody snapped, his tone harsh. "Where are the rest of my friends?"

"They're around," she said. "I'll call the doc."

"No doctor," Brody muttered. "I'm fine." And he slowly sat up.

"No, no, no, you don't," she cried out in alarm.

He glared and ignored her. "I'm getting up," he declared, "and I don't think you are capable of stopping me." Then that voice, the one from his psyche, the one that kept talking to him, the one that called him home, whispered to him.

What about me though? she asked. *I am capable of stopping you.*

He looked around in alarm. "Who said that?"

The nurse looked at him in surprise. "Nobody said anything," she noted cautiously, frowning at him. "That's just a sign that you're not quite back with us yet," she murmured. "Please relax."

He shook his head. "That's not happening," he argued, as he managed to get his legs over the side of the bed. But he was weak; damn, he was weak. He glared as he looked around at the room. "Where am I?"

The nurse looked at him. "I'll call Terk."

"You do that. And tell him to bring me some damn clothes."

And, with that, she took off.

The voice in his head laughed. *Cute,* she said. *You're worrying about your hairy butt after everything you've been through?*

He frowned. "Who the hell are you, and how do you know I've got a hairy butt?"

Because I've seen it, she teased cheerfully. *It's kind of cute too. We'll talk when I get there.*

"No," Brody argued. "I don't know who you are or what

you're doing, but my team is in trouble. I have to go to them. So, if you want to talk, it'll wait until afterward."

This concludes Book 6 of Terkel's Team: Scott's Summit.
Read about Brody's Beast: Terkel's Team, Book 7

Terkel's Team: Brody's Beast (Book #7)

Welcome to a brand-new series from *USA Today* best-selling author Dale Mayer, where dark-ops SEALs have special senses and skills, needed to solve intrigue, betrayal, and ... murder. A series with all the elements you've come to love, plus so much more, ... including psychics!

The journey back to consciousness hadn't been fast or easy but, once awake, with weird images and voices in his head, Brody is all about getting back to the team and into the action. His senses are dulled, but, even then, he's strong enough to know he has to leave the building where he's been recuperating from the initial team accident. Not knowing any of the details doesn't help, but it does mean trust is now *the* issue.

Clary came on board to help when Brody was lost on the ethers—and to help her sister, Cara, who had taken on more than she could handle with Rick's care. And even though Clary had been forewarned as to how this type of connection could work, Clary didn't expect it to work with her and her patient, Brody.

Having a healing pathway was one thing; … having a connection where you could hear thoughts, feel the same emotions, was quite another. And seeing how Brody fights to surmount the attacks on the team he loves so well only shows her how much more is possible—but not the event where she must test out her theory, … unless it's to protect those she cares about.

Find Book 7 here!
To find out more visit Dale Mayer's website.
https://geni.us/DMTTBrodyUniversal

Magnus: Shadow Recon (Book #1)

Deep in the permafrost of the Arctic, a joint task force, comprised of over one dozen countries, comes together to level up their winter skills. A mix of personalities, nationalities, and egos bring out the best—and the worst—as these globally elite men and women work and play together. They rub elbows with hardy locals and a group of scientists gathered close by …

One fatality is almost expected with this training. A second is tough but not a surprise. However, when a third goes missing? It's hard to not be suspicious. When the missing man is connected to one of the elite Maverick team members and is a special friend of Lieutenant Commander Mason Callister? All hell breaks loose …

LIEUTENANT COMMANDER MASON Callister walked into the private office and stood in front of retired Navy Commander Doran Magellan.

"Mason, good to see you."

Yet the dry tone of voice, and the scowl pinching the silver-haired man, all belied his words. Mason had known Doran for over a decade, and their friendship had only grown over time.

Mason waited, as he watched the other man try to work the new tech phone system on his desk. With his hand circling the air above the black box, he appeared to hit buttons randomly.

Mason held back his amusement but to no avail.

"Why can't a phone be a phone anymore?" the commander snapped, as his glare shifted from Mason to the box and back.

Asking the commander if he needed help wouldn't make the older man feel any better, but sitting here and watching as he indiscriminately punched buttons was a struggle. "Is Helen away?" Mason asked.

"Yes, damn it. She's at lunch, and I need her to be at lunch." The commander's piercing gaze pinned Mason in place. "No one is to know you're here."

Solemn, Mason nodded. "Understood."

"Doran? Is that you?" A crotchety voice slammed into the room through the phone's speakers. "Get away from that damn phone. You keep clicking buttons in my ear. Get

Helen in there to do this."

"No, she can't be here for this."

Silence came first, then a huge groan. "Damn it. Then you should have connected me last, so I don't have to sit here and listen to you fumbling around."

"Go pour yourself a damn drink then," Doran barked. "I'm working on the others."

A snort was his only response.

Mason bit the inside of his lip, as he really tried to hold back his grin. The retired commander had been hell on wheels while on active duty, and, even now, the retired part of his life seemed to be more of a euphemism than anything.

"Damn things …"

Mason looked around the dark mahogany office and the walls filled with photos, awards, medals. A life of purpose, accomplishment. And all of that had only piqued his interest during the initial call he'd received, telling him to be here at this time.

"Ah, got it."

Mason's eyebrows barely twitched, as the commander gave him a feral grin. "I'd rather lead a warship into battle than deal with some of today's technology."

As he was one of only a few commanders who'd been in a position to do such a thing, it said much about his capabilities.

And much about current technology.

The commander leaned back in his massive chair and motioned to the cart beside Mason. "Pour three cups."

Interesting. Mason walked a couple steps across the rich tapestry-style carpet and lifted the silver service to pour coffee into three very down-to-earth-looking mugs.

"Black for me."

Mason picked up two cups and walked one over to Doran.

"Thanks." He leaned forward and snapped into the phone, "Everyone here?"

Multiple voices responded.

Curiouser and curiouser. Mason recognized several of the voices. Other relics of an era gone by. Although not a one would like to hear that, and, in good faith, it wasn't fair. Mason had thought each of these men were retired, had relinquished power. Yet, as he studied Doran in front of him, Mason had to wonder if any of them actually had passed the baton or if they'd only slid into the shadows. Was this planned with the government's authority? Or were these retirees a shadow group to the government?

The tangible sense of power and control oozed from Doran's words, tone, stature—his very pores. This man might be heading into his sunset years—based on a simple calculation of chronological years spent on the planet—but he was a long way from being out of the action.

"Mason ..." Doran began.

"Sir?"

"We've got a problem."

Mason narrowed his gaze and waited.

Doran's glare was hard, steely hard, with an icy glint. "Do you know the Mavericks?"

Mason's eyebrows shot up. The black ops division was one of those well-kept secrets, so, therefore, everyone knew about it. He gave a decisive nod. "I do."

"And you're involved in the logistics behind the ICE training program in the Arctic, are you not?"

"I am." Now where was the commander going with this?

"Do you know another SEAL by the name of Mountain

Rode? He's been working for the black ops Mavericks." At his own words, the commander shook his head. "What the hell was his mother thinking when she gave him that moniker?"

"She wasn't thinking anything," said the man with a hard voice from behind Mason.

He stiffened slightly, then relaxed as he recognized that voice too.

"She died giving birth to me. And my full legal name is Mountain Bear Rode. It was my father's doing."

The commander glared at the new arrival. "Did I say you could come in?"

"Yes." Mountain's voice was firm, yet a definitive note of affection filled his tone.

That emotion told Mason so much.

The commander harrumphed, then cleared his throat. "Mason, we're picking up a significant amount of chatter over that ICE training. Most of it good. Some of it the usual caterwauling we've come to expect every time we participate in a joint training mission. This one is set to run for six months, then to reassess."

Mason already knew this. But he waited for the commander to get around to why Mason was here, and, more important, what any of this had to do with the mountain of a man who now towered beside him.

The commander shifted his gaze to Mountain, but he remained silent.

Mason noted Mountain was not only physically big but damn imposing and severely pissed, seemingly barely holding back the forces within. His body language seemed to yell, *And the world will fix this, or I'll find the reason why.*

For a moment Mason felt sorry for the world.

Finally a voice spoke through the phone. "Mason, this is Alpha here. I run the Mavericks. We've got a problem with that ICE training center. Mountain, tell him."

Mason shifted to include Mountain in his field of vision. Mason wished the other men on the conference call were in the room too. It was one thing to deal with men you knew and could take the measure of; it was another when they were silent shadows in the background.

"My brother is one of the men who reported for the Artic training three weeks ago."

"Tergan Rode?" Mason confirmed. "I'm the one who arranged for him to go up there. He's a great kid."

A glimmer of a smile cracked Mountain's stony features. He nodded. "Indeed. A bright light in my often dark world. He's a dozen years younger than me, just passed his BUD/s training this spring, and raring to go. Until his raring to go then got up and went."

Oh, shit. Mason's gaze zinged to the commander, who had kicked up his feet to rest atop the big desk. Stocking feet. With Mickey Mouse images dancing on them. Sidetracked, Mason struggled to pull his attention back to Mountain. "Meaning?"

"He's disappeared." Mountain let out a harsh breath, as if just saying that out loud, and maybe to the right people, could allow him to relax—at least a little.

The commander spoke up. "We need your help, Mason. You're uniquely qualified for this problem."

It didn't sound like he was qualified in any way for anything he'd heard so far. "Clarify." His spoken word was simplicity itself, but the tone behind it said he wanted the cards on the table … now.

Mountain spoke up. "He's the third incident."

Mason's gaze narrowed, as the reports from the training

camp rolled through his mind. "One was Russian. One was from the German SEAL team. Both were deemed accidental deaths."

"No, they weren't."

There it was. The root of the problem in black-and-white. He studied Mountain, aiming for neutrality. "Do you have evidence?"

"My brother did."

"Ah, hell."

Mountain gave a clipped nod. "I'm going to find him."

"Of that I have no doubt," Mason said quietly. "Do you have a copy of the evidence he collected?"

"I have some of it." Mountain held out a USB key. "This is your copy. Top secret."

"We don't have to remind you, Mason, that lives are at stake," Doran added. "Nor do we need another international incident. Consider also that a group of scientists, studying global warming, is close by, and not too far away is a village home to a few hardy locals."

Mason accepted the key, turned to the commander, and asked, "Do we know if this is internal or enemy warfare?"

"We don't know at this point," Alpha replied through the phone. "Mountain will lead Shadow Recon. His mission is twofold. One, find out what's behind these so-called accidents and put a stop to it by any means necessary. Two, locate his brother, hopefully alive."

"And where do I come in?" Mason asked.

"We want you to pull together a special team. The members of Shadow Recon will report to both you and Mountain, just in case."

That was clear enough.

"You'll stay stateside but in constant communication with Mountain—with the caveat that, if necessary, you're on the next flight out."

"What about bringing in other members from the Mavericks?" Mason suggested.

Alpha took this question too, his response coming through via Speakerphone. "We don't have the numbers. The budget for our division has been cut. So we called the commander to pull some strings."

That was Doran's cue to explain further. "Mountain has fought hard to get me on board with this plan, and I'm here now. The navy has a special budget for Shadow Recon and will take care of Mountain and you, Mason, and the team you provide."

"Skills needed?"

"Everything," Mountain said, his voice harsh. "But the biggest is these men need to operate in the shadows, mostly alone, without a team beside them. Too many new arrivals will alert the enemy. If we make any changes to the training program, it will raise alarms. We'll move the men in one or two at a time on the same rotation that the trainees are running right now."

"And when we get to the bottom of this?" Mason looked from the commander back to Mountain.

"Then the training can resume as usual," Doran stated.

Mason immediately churned through the names already popping up in his mind. How much could he tell his men? Obviously not much. Hell, he didn't know much himself. How much time did he have? "Timeline?"

The commander's final word told him of the urgency.

"Yesterday."

Find Magnus here!

To find out more visit Dale Mayer's website.

https://geni.us/DMSRMagnusUniversal

Author's Note

Thank you for reading Scott's Summit: Terkel's Team, Book 6! If you enjoyed the book, please take a moment and leave a short review.

Dear reader,

I love to hear from readers, and you can contact me at my website: www.dalemayer.com or at my Facebook author page. To be informed of new releases and special offers, sign up for my newsletter or follow me on BookBub. And if you are interested in joining Dale Mayer's Reader Group, here is the Facebook sign up page. http://geni.us/DaleMayerFBGroup

Cheers,
Dale Mayer

Get THREE Free Books Now!

Have you met the SEALS of Honor?

SEALs of Honor Books 1, 2, and 3. Follow the stories of brave, badass warriors who serve their country with honor and love their women to the limits of life and death.

Read Mason, Hawk, and Dane right now for FREE.

Go here and tell me where to send them!
https://dalemayer.com/masonfree

About the Author

Dale Mayer is a *USA Today* best-selling author, best known for her SEALs military romances, her Psychic Visions series, and her Lovely Lethal Garden cozy series. Her contemporary romances are raw and full of passion and emotion (Broken But … Mending, Hathaway House series). Her thrillers will keep you guessing (Kate Morgan, By Death series), and her romantic comedies will keep you giggling (*It's a Dog's Life*, a stand-alone novella; and the Broken Protocols series, starring Charming Marvin, the cat).

Dale honors the stories that come to her—and some of them are crazy, break all the rules and cross multiple genres!

To go with her fiction, she also writes nonfiction in many different fields, with books available on résumé writing, companion gardening, and the US mortgage system. All her books are available in print and ebook format.

Connect with Dale Mayer Online

Dale's Website – www.dalemayer.com
Twitter – @DaleMayer
Facebook Page – geni.us/DaleMayerFBFanPage
Facebook Group – geni.us/DaleMayerFBGroup
BookBub – geni.us/DaleMayerBookbub
Instagram – geni.us/DaleMayerInstagram
Goodreads – geni.us/DaleMayerGoodreads
Newsletter – geni.us/DaleNews

Also by Dale Mayer

Published Adult Books:

Shadow Recon
Magnus, Book 1

Bullard's Battle
Ryland's Reach, Book 1
Cain's Cross, Book 2
Eton's Escape, Book 3
Garret's Gambit, Book 4
Kano's Keep, Book 5
Fallon's Flaw, Book 6
Quinn's Quest, Book 7
Bullard's Beauty, Book 8
Bullard's Best, Book 9
Bullard's Battle, Books 1–2
Bullard's Battle, Books 3–4
Bullard's Battle, Books 5–6
Bullard's Battle, Books 7–8

Terkel's Team
Damon's Deal, Book 1
Wade's War, Book 2
Gage's Goal, Book 3
Calum's Contact, Book 4
Rick's Road, Book 5

Scott's Summit, Book 6
Brody's Beast, Book 7

Kate Morgan
Simon Says... Hide, Book 1
Simon Says... Jump, Book 2
Simon Says... Ride, Book 3
Simon Says... Scream, Book 4
Simon Says... Run, Book 5

Hathaway House
Aaron, Book 1
Brock, Book 2
Cole, Book 3
Denton, Book 4
Elliot, Book 5
Finn, Book 6
Gregory, Book 7
Heath, Book 8
Iain, Book 9
Jaden, Book 10
Keith, Book 11
Lance, Book 12
Melissa, Book 13
Nash, Book 14
Owen, Book 15
Percy, Book 16
Quinton, Book 17
Ryatt, Book 18
Hathaway House, Books 1–3
Hathaway House, Books 4–6
Hathaway House, Books 7–9

The K9 Files

Lovely Lethal Gardens

Gun in the Gardenias, Book 7
Handcuffs in the Heather, Book 8
Ice Pick in the Ivy, Book 9
Jewels in the Juniper, Book 10
Killer in the Kiwis, Book 11
Lifeless in the Lilies, Book 12
Murder in the Marigolds, Book 13
Nabbed in the Nasturtiums, Book 14
Offed in the Orchids, Book 15
Poison in the Pansies, Book 16
Quarry in the Quince, Book 17
Revenge in the Roses, Book 18
Silenced in the Sunflowers, Book 19
Lovely Lethal Gardens, Books 1–2
Lovely Lethal Gardens, Books 3–4
Lovely Lethal Gardens, Books 5–6
Lovely Lethal Gardens, Books 7–8
Lovely Lethal Gardens, Books 9–10

Psychic Vision Series

Tuesday's Child
Hide 'n Go Seek
Maddy's Floor
Garden of Sorrow
Knock Knock…
Rare Find
Eyes to the Soul
Now You See Her
Shattered
Into the Abyss
Seeds of Malice
Eye of the Falcon

Itsy-Bitsy Spider
Unmasked
Deep Beneath
From the Ashes
Stroke of Death
Ice Maiden
Snap, Crackle…
What If…
Talking Bones
String of Tears
Psychic Visions Books 1–3
Psychic Visions Books 4–6
Psychic Visions Books 7–9

By Death Series
Touched by Death
Haunted by Death
Chilled by Death
By Death Books 1–3

Broken Protocols – Romantic Comedy Series
Cat's Meow
Cat's Pajamas
Cat's Cradle
Cat's Claus
Broken Protocols 1-4

Broken and… Mending
Skin
Scars
Scales (of Justice)
Broken but… Mending 1-3

Glory

Genesis
Tori
Celeste
Glory Trilogy

Biker Blues

Morgan: Biker Blues, Volume 1
Cash: Biker Blues, Volume 2

SEALs of Honor

Mason: SEALs of Honor, Book 1
Hawk: SEALs of Honor, Book 2
Dane: SEALs of Honor, Book 3
Swede: SEALs of Honor, Book 4
Shadow: SEALs of Honor, Book 5
Cooper: SEALs of Honor, Book 6
Markus: SEALs of Honor, Book 7
Evan: SEALs of Honor, Book 8
Mason's Wish: SEALs of Honor, Book 9
Chase: SEALs of Honor, Book 10
Brett: SEALs of Honor, Book 11
Devlin: SEALs of Honor, Book 12
Easton: SEALs of Honor, Book 13
Ryder: SEALs of Honor, Book 14
Macklin: SEALs of Honor, Book 15
Corey: SEALs of Honor, Book 16
Warrick: SEALs of Honor, Book 17
Tanner: SEALs of Honor, Book 18
Jackson: SEALs of Honor, Book 19
Kanen: SEALs of Honor, Book 20
Nelson: SEALs of Honor, Book 21

Taylor: SEALs of Honor, Book 22

Colton: SEALs of Honor, Book 23

Troy: SEALs of Honor, Book 24

Axel: SEALs of Honor, Book 25

Baylor: SEALs of Honor, Book 26

Hudson: SEALs of Honor, Book 27

Lachlan: SEALs of Honor, Book 28

Paxton: SEALs of Honor, Book 29

SEALs of Honor, Books 1–3

SEALs of Honor, Books 4–6

SEALs of Honor, Books 7–10

SEALs of Honor, Books 11–13

SEALs of Honor, Books 14–16

SEALs of Honor, Books 17–19

SEALs of Honor, Books 20–22

SEALs of Honor, Books 23–25

Heroes for Hire

Levi's Legend: Heroes for Hire, Book 1

Stone's Surrender: Heroes for Hire, Book 2

Merk's Mistake: Heroes for Hire, Book 3

Rhodes's Reward: Heroes for Hire, Book 4

Flynn's Firecracker: Heroes for Hire, Book 5

Logan's Light: Heroes for Hire, Book 6

Harrison's Heart: Heroes for Hire, Book 7

Saul's Sweetheart: Heroes for Hire, Book 8

Dakota's Delight: Heroes for Hire, Book 9

Tyson's Treasure: Heroes for Hire, Book 10

Jace's Jewel: Heroes for Hire, Book 11

Rory's Rose: Heroes for Hire, Book 12

Brandon's Bliss: Heroes for Hire, Book 13

Liam's Lily: Heroes for Hire, Book 14

SEALs of Steel

SEALs of Steel, Books 1–4
SEALs of Steel, Books 5–8
SEALs of Steel, Books 1–8

The Mavericks

Kerrick, Book 1
Griffin, Book 2
Jax, Book 3
Beau, Book 4
Asher, Book 5
Ryker, Book 6
Miles, Book 7
Nico, Book 8
Keane, Book 9
Lennox, Book 10
Gavin, Book 11
Shane, Book 12
Diesel, Book 13
Jerricho, Book 14
Killian, Book 15
Hatch, Book 16
Corbin, Book 17
Aiden, Book 18
The Mavericks, Books 1–2
The Mavericks, Books 3–4
The Mavericks, Books 5–6
The Mavericks, Books 7–8
The Mavericks, Books 9–10
The Mavericks, Books 11–12

Collections

Dare to Be You...

Dare to Love…
Dare to be Strong…
RomanceX3

Standalone Novellas
It's a Dog's Life
Riana's Revenge
Second Chances

Published Young Adult Books:

Family Blood Ties Series
Vampire in Denial
Vampire in Distress
Vampire in Design
Vampire in Deceit
Vampire in Defiance
Vampire in Conflict
Vampire in Chaos
Vampire in Crisis
Vampire in Control
Vampire in Charge
Family Blood Ties Set 1–3
Family Blood Ties Set 1–5
Family Blood Ties Set 4–6
Family Blood Ties Set 7–9
Sian's Solution, A Family Blood Ties Series Prequel
     Novelette

Design series
Dangerous Designs
Deadly Designs

Darkest Designs
Design Series Trilogy

Standalone

In Cassie's Corner
Gem Stone (a Gemma Stone Mystery)
Time Thieves

Published Non-Fiction Books:

Career Essentials

Career Essentials: The Résumé
Career Essentials: The Cover Letter
Career Essentials: The Interview
Career Essentials: 3 in 1

www.ingramcontent.com/pod-product-compliance
Lightning Source LLC
Chambersburg PA
CBHW071436200726

48294CB00002B/666